Paul Shivell

Ashes of Roses

Paul Shivell

Ashes of Roses

ISBN/EAN: 9783337420079

Printed in Europe, USA, Canada, Australia, Japan

Cover: Foto ©Andreas Hilbeck / pixelio.de

More available books at **www.hansebooks.com**

DEDICATION.

This is my book.   I come to you, my father,
  And for the disobedience of past years
I ask forgiveness.   We have loved together,
  And quenched the bonfires of my youth with tears,
Yet I grow full: the old wrong reappears;
  And I must be assured once more with kindness
That you still love me,—that the wound endears
  Thy son, who gave it, for 't was all in blindness.

This is my book.   Oh can you feel the pride
You felt that evening by the riverside,
  When with emotion a good father knows,
You heard me read my little piece, September,
  Written that day, my first developed rose,
The one you loved the most.—do you remember?

Contents

Contents

Contents

Contents

Ashes of Roses

SEPTEMBER.

September's sun stole softly on the land,
Peeped 'tween the crags, and bathed the glittering
    sand,
Where, 'neath the cliff, the fishing hamlet lay,
In dreamy silence of another day.

The night's sweet dew, in morn's thin mist set free,
Was wafted on the zephyrs out to sea ;
Where white-winged ships, against a cloudless sky,
Leaned in the breeze, and drifted slowly by.

From where the spray fell sparkling at their feet,
The loving fishwives watched the little fleet.
Still, lingering slow along the sobbing shore,
Wiped 'way their tears to view the specks once more.

Soon, from their cheerful huts, their hopeful lays
Of Time Eternal, and its brighter days,
Stole sweetly on the silence of the morn,
And fainted in the breeze the night had borne.

The village children, fresh from restful sleep,
Had scrambled up the rocks, and down the steep,
And chased each other on across the sand,
Exchanging screams with sea-birds as they ran.

Still, from their distant play-ground in the shade
Of some tall cliff, for drowsy echoes made,
Their mirthful voices sweetly rose and fell,
And distant sea-birds screamed their sad farewell.

So dreamed the early morn into the past,
That will absorb all earthly time at last;
When all the joys and sorrows of life's day
Will fade in sleep's forgetfulness away.

Thus will the Muse of humble poets sing
Each morn's delights—and each its own will bring—
To all true lovers of life's simple charms,
Till Time and Fate resound their last alarms.

WATCHING A SHIP AT SEA.

Dream on, O silent ship, dream on and on.
Here by this peaceful sea, at quiet dawn,
A little child, in the joy of health,
I'll plan a life of greatness for myself.
I'll build a mighty ship and sail the seas!
Or help the aged to a life of ease.
I'll build white cities by the ocean's shore!
Or journey through the land and help the poor.
I'll wed a little girl and live in state!
But shall not turn the hungry from my gate.
And while I walk with Jesus all life long,
I'll dream with thee, O silent ship; dream on.

Dream on, O silent ship, dream on and on.
The morning mists flee fast before the sun.

2

And life in clearer view before me lies
Than I had seen through childhood's glorious eyes.
But in the hideous turmoil of the war
Of man 'gainst man, in greed of pomp and store,
I shall not enter; but with brother's love,
In harmony with that of Heaven above,
I'll have a kindly hand and happy word
To succor the oppressed, and comfort those who've
      erred.
So, on through serious life with cheerful song,
I'll dream with thee, O silent ship; dream on.

Dream on, O silent ship, dream on and on.
The graver calls of life are now begun.
For my beloved need the bread of life,
And I must humbly enter in the strife.
But Nature for her children will provide,
If they'll but throw vain fantasy aside,
And live by product of a fruitful brain,
Or till the sunny soil, made sweet with wind and rain.
So I will live, and humbly earn the bread,
Which then our God will give, as Christ hath said.
Then when at eve I rest, my labor done,
I'll dream with thee, O silent ship; dream on.

Dream on, O silent ship, dream on and on.
The fruits of eager toil are now my own.
My faithful ones, the few that do not sleep
Upon the silent hill above the deep,
Enjoy the pleasures of abundance given
To those who follow the precepts of Heaven.

And I, who've followed in the paths I made
In morning life, now lie in noon-life's shade;
And muse with vague regret upon the past,
Or contemplate the sweetness of my last;
While still I harvest life's poetic lawn,
And dream with thee, O silent ship; dream on.

Dream on, O silent ship, dream on and on.
Still evening with its train comes stealing on.
Thy spreading wake laps faintly on the shore,
And the receding past is heard no more.
And I, alone beside this quiet sea,
Where I have dreamed these many years with thee.
Await the time when God shall call me home,
To dream forever where no storms shall come.
But others here, when I at last am gone,
Will dream with thee, O silent ship; dream on.

Dream on, O silent ship, dream on and on;
The boundless deep is all thy happy home;
Whose restless bosom holds the ebbing day,
That soon, with me, will fade and pass away.
When night, that follows on the setting sun,
Will lie within the deep as day has done,
And, fleeing from the morn, will oft return
With rest for souls like me, that watch and yearn.

Now darkness flows upon the ebbing light:
The sea reflects the fast-increasing night.
Thy airy sails, like night mist o'er my soul,
Speed me away beyond the world's control—

4

A light! A light! far on the dim sea-line
It brightens, broadens, and goes out.   Not mine.
But, though I linger, I shall soon be gone.
I cannot see.   But thou, O silent ship, speed on.

BITTERNESS AND FAITH.

I.

There are no good.   Go mount the peak
    And see life's farther surge.
See darkness reeked in horror sneak
    Along the scowling verge,
And storms through all like dragons crawl,
    Wild-anxious to emerge.

Look not for joy in this bleak world,
    Where thorns guard every rose,
Where serpents creep through broken sleep
    In beds of friendly foes;
For hideous screams will end thy dreams
    When Death's wings round thee close.

For all the world's an empty glass,
    From which the foolish drink,
And o'er their sips they smack their lips,
    And never pause to think,
While wise men stand aloof and pass
    Around the knowing wink.

5

II.

Ah, Bitterness, men may be wrong,
   But they are nearest right
Who find no fault, but with a song
   Turn misery to delight.
And they are least who at their feast
   Have Ridicule and Spite.

THE SEA.

Blow, blow, breezes, blow!
Over the dripping waves we go,
Out of the bay and into the dawn,
Where the dew lies cool on the ocean lawn,—
Oh! our life's as free as the vagrant sea—
Sing! who can tell what to-morrow will be?
Up with the sky, boys! Steady, steady,
And the dizzy waters spiral and eddy
Into the wake as we gurgle along,
Wind and waves and bubble and song,
Over the sprawling foam we go,—
Blow, blow, breezes, blow!

Away, away to the open sea!
Swift as the gull in the wind are we.
Cheerily, cheerily, on we go,
With the wet sky drowned in the sea below,—
Oh! we challenge aloud to the mountainous cloud,
And away we cut with our gun'ales bowed—
Up, up, down, down,
With a sternward glimpse of the far-off town;

Hurrily, drowsily, on we fly,
With the driving cloud in the whistling sky.
Far from the pent-up world are we,
Headed out to the open sea.

SOLITUDE.

Ah, it was dreamy weather.
   The summer sea at evening lay asleep.
We sat alone together,
   And heard with beating hearts the long swells creep
Along the silent shore,
That echoed back our promise, "Evermore."

A year of nights has flown;
   And still the sea in nature's bosom sleeps.
All yearningly alone
   I listen: and the same cold swell still creeps
From that Eternal Shore,
But answers me: "No, never; nevermore."

EQUATORIA.

Here the torrid heaven glitters away
   To a palm-line, dimly seen,
Returning again, ruffled now and then,
   In the lake that glares between.
Deep, deep, deep
   Is the lurid tropic sky,

And deeper the green in the smoothe lake's sheen
 Where the languid lilies lie.
Far down the skies,
 Where the hot horizon lies,
By the low, green neck I can see a speck,
Dark, like the smoke from a burning wreck,
 And a lonely sea-bird cries.

All glare and dead lies the glassy lake,
 And stark stand the breathless trees.
No beast nor bird to be seen or heard:
 No sound from the dying breeze.
Hot, hot, hot
 Is the burning tropic sky.
All stagnant the green in the poisonous sheen,
 Where the lilies droop and die.
Far, far away,
 Like a wild beast of prey,
The dark cyclone comes forth alone
 From the verge of the molten day.

All still and hot lies the gloomy lake,
 Where the lilies gasp for breath;
And the great heart-beat of the world of heat
 Is held in the hush of death.
All, all around,
 No stir,—no sign of a sound;
And the sickly swoon of the wide lagoon,
 And the wide, wide world profound,
And the beat, beat, beat,
 Of the merciless, pitiless heat,

Ashes 𝔬𝔣 Roses

And the weird, wild moan of the dark cyclone,
   Like a plague in a winding sheet,—

Up from suspense starts the shuddering air,
   And away from the haunted lake,
On ghostly wings, like imagined things
   In the lull of a midnight wake.
On, on, on
   Comes the panting, groaning cloud,
Twisting the lake till its waters break,
   And seethe, and bellow aloud.
Night! night! night!
   Oh, God! what a gloomy sight—
The place—the place—Oh, fierce embrace
Of the blinding, stifling—Ah, a space,
And the sun bursts forth with steaming face
On the blessed scene,—God's love—God's grace—
   Breathe! while the air is light.

All fresh and cool flows the laughing lake,
   Bringing the deep blue sky,
And peaceful and calm stands the graceful palm,
   Where the wheeling storm-birds cry.
Hush! hush! hush!
   Oh, hush to the throne of God!
All scattered the green where the ripples careen,
   Lapping the lily pods.
Far, far across,
   Where the sparkling whitecaps toss,
White birds of peace from their hidings cease,
And on in the glimmering world's decrease
   Goes the wandering albatross.

SUMMER NIGHT.

Oh, I hear music! While I hold my breath,
    Listening, afar it seems,
As when the strange return of friends from death
    Hangs in the sad uncertainty of dreams.
Woo me from sleeping, — rouse me with soft strains
    To sweeter visions, where the enchanted lay
Lingers and lingers while the night remains,
    And I may die in tune and float away.
Oh, melody of sweet sounds that love to well
    From silence, and live on!
My soul gropes out into the night: thy spell
Lures with untruthful echoes that do tell
    Sweeter than truth. I feel the breath of dawn
Born of a night of music. Hark! One swell,—
And all is silent now, and thou art gone.

THE DEAD YEAR.

The year we loved is dead: see where she lies,
    Cold, and still beautiful, in her shroud of snow.
The sun, withdrawn behind the moaning skies,
    No more with beaming face sees joy o'erflow.
    The flowers that in his love-glance blushed to blow,
Bowed down with sorrow, closed their withered eyes.
    The brook is silent where we loved to go,
And, for it hears no sound, the hill no more replies.

Ah, we remember since that life is flown,
    And through the fields with her no more we rove,

How all the fair young flowers, bereaved and lone,
  Would sadly watch for some responsive love;
And how they missed the sun's face from above,
And saw the darkening clouds where he had shone;
  And how deep in the wood the mateless dove
Sighed to the mournful, gathering cold alone.

Ah, long they listened for that blither note
  Of happy lark, or for the long love strain
That sweetened from the sylvan warbler's throat
  To thrill an answer from his mate again.
  Ah, long they listened; but they harked in vain;
And heard but voices of the forest float
  Out o'er the unheeding sea, and there complain
Of death, death, death,—'till life was death by rote.

Oft when the stricken sun still slowly crept,
  They watched and waited for his old love-light.
Through many a faded day their vigil kept,
  Till storms of icy tears bedimmed their sight.
  Then as the dreary days gave way to lengthened
      night,
And the cold, cheerless hours in silence wept,
  The stalwart trees, in grief, relaxed their might,
And gave their leaves to warm the flowers that slept.

And then by night from out the gloom and chill,
  Wierd funeral trains of grief-crazed birds sped on,
Away forever in far clouds, and still
  There followed more when their dark forms were
      gone.

And through the shivering night the orphan fawn
Crouched in the brake beside the querulous rill;
 Or watched the cold, gray moonlight on the lawn,
When the north wind's sorrow swooned, and all was
  still.

The year we loved is dead.   Come where she lies,
 Cold, and still beautiful, on her couch of snow.
Come let us hurry where the brooding skies
 Comfort the sighing winds with kindred woe.
 Come where the frozen brook has ceased to flow,
And the cold, voiceless cliff no more replies.
 Come where the lovely year lies dead below,
And look beyond the world to Him who never dies.

FRAGMENTS TO MYSELF.

When fools reprove thee for a foolish act,
 Be not consoled to think they have not wit;
But, clothed in all the honest glare of fact,
 Know if thy garb appropriately fit.
Perchance, in wisdom of thine own conceit,
Thou sittest, an arch-fool, at thy folly's feet.

A child instructs thee: thy impatient pride
 Cuts him short off, as if thou comprehend;
He learns thy silly weakness, and beside,
 What hast thou gained by ignorance of his end?
'T were better far to hear a child advise,
Than cut him off to seem, thyself, more wise.

If one should ask thee to impart to him
  Uncommon knowledge, simply aquiesce,
And humbly fill his question to the brim,
  Giving the truth in words of gentle stress.
Impart, and find thy pleasure in the end
That he who asks is happy to attend.

Hear all the teachings of the great.
  Ev'n profit by the fool.
Toil on, nor stop to imitate,
  Nor bind thyself by rule.
In thine own state originate
  A new and better school.

Be sure your conversation's such
That, talking little, you say much.

THE CANNON.

This is the gun whose iron mouth
  Belched shrieking death and loud destruction forth,
Tore the fierce vitals from the struggling South,
  And bound it to the North.

No more around thy starlit throne
  The dead shall lie, the dying writhe in pain;
Nor where the wild war bugle shall be blown
  Thy voice be heard again.

Back in that dark and empty cell,
  Where crouched the awful substance of thy wrath,
The busy sparrows build their nests and dwell,
  And block the smoothe-worn path.

Sleep, monster of the stripes and stars ;
  Thy bellowing voice the voice of God hath stilled.
Let us forget the memory of old wars ;
  Come ye, and let us build.

Come let us love, and build, and teach,
  Till white and black shall issue from the past,
And through the blend of nations we shall reach
  The peaceful truth at last.

DREAMING.

The sky above is clear and blue.
The sea is of a softer hue.
And far out in the mists they meet and hide from
    view.

There, whitened in the morning sun,
A single sail allures me on
To dream of happier days, grown sad since they are
    gone.

I care not for the heaven that's told,
Of gates of pearl and streets of gold,
But just such place to meet my friends when I am old.

DAWN.

One morn, God's peace was with me, when I strolled
Across the fields, beside the summer wood.
High o'er the glistening oaks the gold-tinged clouds
Clasped hands to welcome forth the blushing dawn ;
When, from the quiet of that summer morn,
All nature sang the glory of our God.
From the bright fields, where flowers laughed with dew,
The cool, green wood, the brook, and halloed hill—
All in the freshness of the morning air—
Yea, from the very soul of all the earth,
Swelled the high anthem that not men alone,
But all God's works, do feel a thrill to hear.
Birds sang till e'en the jay tuned well his note,
And joined the anthem with the dove.   Beneath,
Sweet robins in unruly choirs filled
The grove and meadow with their summer song.
And I, in the spirit of the joyful time,
Joined soul and voice, and lifting up my praise
To Him who blessed me with a life so full
Of sympathy, with all that He has made,
Clapped hands for joy !   Oh, I was happy then.

PRIMITIVE THEOLOGY.

"De hya'bes' is ready !   But de reapahs is few."
Whaffo' you a-sayin' dah's nuffin' to do?
Does you s'pose to go loafin' de long wintah thue?
Does you 'spec's de Lawd's guine to keep black folks
      lak you?

Git out on de highways an' fetchin' dem in!
Don' say dat means preachahs; dat's gittin' too thin.
Hyeah's 'nough lazy sinnahs fu' to mek de wu'k spin!
An' dey's only one time, an' dat's now! So bergin!

Hey! You in de gall'ry! Cain't you leave off awhile?
Dis ain' no place fu' you-all youngstahs to smile.
Brethern, open yo' eyes! an' see mile on mile
Ob human watah mell'ns 'bout ready to spile!

Den tol' me dis ain' no time fu' to wu'k?
Dat's all mighty fine fu' you sinnahs dat shirk.
But de debil is in you, and dah he will lurk,
Twell de all-seein' Lawd gins a wink to his clerk,

An' he says to his clerk, says'e: Buil' me a fiah!
As high as de highes' chu'ch steeple an' highah!
'Twell I burn ebry drone right along wiv de liah,
Don' keer ef he's preachah, o' deacon, o' squiah!

An' den de nex' minute, afo' you kin tell,
You'll be chucked in de fiah an' brimstone ob hell!
An' when yo' own meat in de cookin' you smell,
Dah's de time fu' to holler, an' shoutin' an' yell.

An' you'll call to de Lawd, an' you'll 'low "Lookee
        hyeah!
Recollec' how I sarbed you an' moved in yo' feah?"
An' de debil'll fork you and 'low wiv a sneah:
"Any man dat's got time to spah ortn't to keer."

Den's when to wa'm up yo' religion an' scream.
But all yo' salt watah'll tu'n into steam.

16

An' you won' come to, fu' it ain't no dream,
But de fac's, as dey is in dis hyeah Book—de cream!

Now s'pose, on de othah han', yo an' yo' kin
Snatchin' all yo' brethern an' sistern f'um sin,—
Not stan' roun' de chu'ch do' a-axin' dem in,—
Git out on de highways and waggle yo' chin!

An' when you's done thue instahcatin' yo' search,
An' cram-flll de benches an' cheers in dis chu'ch,
You'll be sho' ob yo' wings, an' yo' hyahp, an' yo'
      perch,
Fo' de Lawd nevah leave hustlin' man in de lurch.

An' you'll hyeah de Lawd tell his clerk: "Dem lazy
      mans,
What ust ter set on de yarth holdin' dey han's,
Is learnt bettah sense, f'um de way de count stan's,
So we'll jes' leave 'em in to de great Promis' Lan's."

An' den when dat clerk rolls dem bright eyes erbout,
An' commences fu' flllin' dem blank tickets out,
Dah'll be heap plenty time fu' you sinnahs to shout,
An' talk 'bout yo' neighbah dat's bein' locked out.

CHILDREN.

Please, sister, sit beside my bed,
   And hold my fingers tight;
Please put your arm around my head,
   I feel so sad to-night.

I never feel so happy, dear,
As when we had our mamma here.
I loved my mamma, Oh, so much,
And loved to feel her gentle touch,
Like when she used to lay my hair
Back from my eyes and kiss me there.
And kiss you then.   Oh sister dear,
I wish we had our mamma here.

Don't cry, sister, —please don't cry.
   Some day we'll go up there,
Way up to Heaven in the sky,
   'Cause mamma told me where.
When she was sick that's what she said,
When I was staying by her bed.
She told me pretty stories, too,
About how little flowers grew,
And how the birdies have to go
In winter; 'cause she talked so low,
And looked at me, and then I cried.
And then she kissed me,—and mamma died.

DEDICATION FOR SCHOOL ANNUAL.

How school days lengthen out life's youthful Spring,
And keep the health that youthful pleasures bring.
How we, in thoughtlessness of foolish hours,
Sow in life's early field these wilder flowers;
These weeds of idle thought, which, having reaped,
And bound in sheaves, we give you now to keep.
May they, dead wild flowers in life's sober field,
Forever keep the fickle scent they yield.

A FRAGMENT.

While I have life, I'll live to bless those lives
That know of mine, by being known for deeds
That all will love, and loving, will be happy.
By wise activity to leave the world
The lovelier for my having tarried in it.
This is my aim.   I shall apply myself
To such pursuits as call my nobler parts
To worthy exercise.   God give me grace.

THE ARTIST AND THE ARTISAN: AN ESSAY.

First Means Prize, Phillips Academy, Andover,
1895.

One word may stand for others, when alone,
Which, placed with others, takes some shade or tone;
But, used too often in so many ways,
The finer meaning's lost; the coarser stays.
Thus, vulgar associations have combined,
To make our noble theme sound unrefined;
For "artist" means most any artful man,
Who, rudely skilled, is called an artisan.
'Tis here our object, by a just defense,
To throw some light upon the finer sense.
First, of the artist, born by Heaven's decree,
To tell emotions none have felt as he;
Whose lightest thoughts are finer thoughts than ours,
And, clothed by him, express resistless powers:
Still, through whose deeper musings ever gleams

19

His chosen light, reflecting all he dreams.
See where he goes to hail the charms that lie
In clouds becalmed, or in the wind-swept sky !
There, ever rising with his chosen Muse,
To make immortal what his soul may choose :
Forever seeking heights that none attain,
Soars from the theme that we have tried in vain ;
And, quitting earthly for ethereal laws,
Wins from the world a weak, but just, applause.
Shall we, whose love he earns with works so dear,
Rate low the man, if he should blunder here?
If worldly weak, how recompensed to show
What we of worldly strength might never know.
Diviner inspirations from above
Echo to us, from him, diviner love.
His sigh, or smile, or deeply boisterous laugh,
Will find in us, who understand not half,
Some faint response, which in itself shall wake
Our quivering heart-strings for a nobler sake.
 O'er some strong means he must some mastery
  gain,
Else all these higher flights would be in vain ;
But none so poor is sent to teach mankind,
But God has given to him the proper mind ;
Which, rightly trained, may master what it will,
As means to greater end than show of skill.
So great that end, that, to obscure the means,
Is art of art, and merits as it gains.
 Musician, painter, poet, — what the name —
By different means will all express the same ;
And, though we may not read them as we run,

The two, imagined, may reveal the one.
As when breathless Appreciation stands
Before the "Angelus," nor understands
What it may be in that rude peasant pair
Foils his weak speech:—'t is God keeps silence there.
Beneath he reads the poet's simple word:
"Still, when the night is come, praise ye the Lord."
He listens:—faintly from the distant tower
Celestial chimes melt in the holy hour;
The radiant clouds still follow on the sun,
And twilight steals across:—the day is done.
    The artist, to create this charm, employed
The simplest symbols, lest it be destroyed:
His deeper feelings he did so suggest,
That we might see the thought, and feel the rest.
But had he wished that lovelier charm to fail,
He'd but to drown it in a skilled detail.
For who has taste for overdrawn accounts
Of what suggestion had made clear at once?
And who but loves to feel he comprehends
The final point before the story ends?
Thus, to the portrait of a dearest friend,
Well-painted flesh no natural feelings lend:
We look for well-remembered traits that lie
Drawn in the mouth, or twinkling in the eye;
He who denies us this most fair delight,
And seeks to please us merely through our sight,
Showing us clearly what we clearly saw,
To show us how precisely he can draw,—
Is but an artisan, and, master of his art,
May please the mind, but never charm the heart.

The rhetorician may, with skill, define
Unwieldy things in but a single line;
And, when the charms are spent, and praises few,
Play on his words, and catch with something new.
Or, if good style in some great work he sees,
He launches forth in that same style to please;
Till lack of finer power soon has shown
The art he tried to copy not his own.
For, as 'tis genius does what none can do,
The artisan cannot be artist too.
Unless, unsuited to his motive here,
He mounts, an artist, to his native sphere;
Where, though by training he's a craftsman still,
His motive, changed, is higher now than skill.
But both are skilled in the same art to show,
This, what he feels, that, what he's proud to know.
As skill was first in rank when art began,
The artist first must be an artisan;
But, artist-born, he soon or late will soar,
However fettered by his craft before.
　　Then let the artisan his mastery tell,
That he of greater power may use it well.
Then when we drink the joys of sweeter song;
Of deeper truth, that never can be wrong;
Of nobler thoughts, more masterfully told;
Of purer love, that never shall grow old:
We'll crown the heaven-born genius in the skies,
And honor him who helped his soul to rise.

MELODRAMA.

The glims were doused throughout the house,
  Except the dim footlights.
The fiddles whined the tune you'll find
  Whene'er the villian fights.

The murderous-toned bass viol groaned,
  Low-voiced and full of rage,
When, knives in hand, the robber band
  Sneaked in upon the stage.

Their bright knives glistened; they paused and listened;
  Then flourished, breathed, and glared.
Now puffed and boiled, lunged and recoiled,
  Folded their arms and stared.

The painted streaks upon their cheeks
  Frightened, repulsed, defied!
Each clenched his fist and scowled and hissed,
  And muttered oaths aside.

The thunder crashed!   The lightning flashed
  And lighted up the gloom!
They tore their hair in dire despair,
  And bit their teeth at doom.

Like vicious men, they breathed again,
  And whipped into a rage!
Then, turning round, without a sound,
  They sneaked across the stage.

IN AN OLD BOOK ON LEAVING SCHOOL.

While grinding through these tattered pages
For Charlie, Goat, and other sages,
Remember him who now engages
    In what he pleases,
Far from their dull scholastic cages
    And brain diseases.

EPISTLE TO LAIRD EASTON.

Laird Easton, Flunk, Andover, Mass.,
Who, on a dog's-eared Latin ass,
Prepares to chill the Middle Class
    With one bold stagger:—
Say, don't you know you'll never pass,
    You tough old swagger?

You awkward old ungainly, slow,
Good-natured, easy, generous flow
Of soul, what are you up to? Ho!
    Or are you up yet?
I don't believe you are, by Joe!
    But I won't stop yet.

East! East! Get up you snorting beastie!
You mind me of a drunk-fat priestie,
Rolled up so careless-like and resty
    Beneath the cover,—
Get up! You hear me? Ho there! Eastie!
    That's right, turn over.

Ashes of Roses

East! East! You lazy, dark-complected,
Eternal snoozer, grin-infected.
And always, when awake, expected
       To act the fool,—
Get up and get your brains collected!—
       It's time for school!

Sleep on, sleep on, thou noble sleeper.
Sleep on, and dream of sleep yet deeper.
East! East! Look! quick! here goes a creeper
       Straight up your nose!
There, now, get up and rub your weepers,
       And hunt your clo'es.

Give ear unto my awkward lay.—
What's that you were about to say?
You're tired? Why certainly, you jay,
       When were you not tired
Since that long, prehistoric day
       When first you got tired?

Come, East, my dear old patient friend,
And if you've got the time to spend,
Just prop your eyelids and attend
       To my descriptions.
Come, you must hear me to the end,—
       None your conniptions.

I'll soon be rhyming at a rate
That often gets me in debate,

For wiser folks warn me to wait
  Until I'm older,
And, in the meantime, educate
  With some mind-molder.

But Eastie, I have had enough
Of this long-faced pedantic bluff,
With time-dried tongues, and all such stuff,
  So, for awhile,
I'll be contented with my rough,
  Untutored style.

And why should I be made to climb
Head downward through the caves of time,
My tired brain groping in the grime
  Of book and bone,
While far above, the clear sublime
  Dreams on alone?

If God made me to tell the tale
That lingers in the scented gale,
Or lights the fast-receding sail
  Far out at sea,
Then sea and meadow, hill and vale,
  Are books for me.

He who inspired me not to stay,
Who hears the music of my lay,
Will guide me on my erring way,
  As I ascend,

Ashes of Roses

Till sweetly at the close of day,
    My song shall end.

Who'd bask in Goat's unwholesome graces
Must truckle in the proper places;
Not flush with feeling's honest faces,
    But haste to choke
With well-forced mirth and strained grimaces
    At every joke.

And oh, how hard to counterfeit
Conviction of a startling hit,
When pity for the weakling wit
    Sickens the grin,
Till all our face spells "hypocrite"
    From hair to chin.

The poor, deluded, greasy grind,
Who dotes upon a book-stuffed mind,
And plugs his Latin till he's blind
    With brute tenacity,
In hearts like these will always find
    Enough capacity.

But he who lives by inspiration,
And seeks a means in education,
Instead of a bookworm occupation
    Of deep research,
Though abler, knows no approbation
    From school or church.

Ashes of Roses

And so there languished a poor prep,
Who joked, and read, and laughed, and slept,
And got his lessons well, except
    When wasting time,
Against the English prof's precept,
    In writing rhyme.

No more that master's keen insight
Shall pierce the literary night,
And drag his victim forth to light:
    Mind is dominion!
Behold I exercise my write,
    Nor ask opinion.

I left.   I was uncomprehended
As for some special life intended,
And feared my dreams would soon be ended
    With sneering tutors.
But I regret that I offended
    My persecutors.

But in that grinding anchoret
I found one friend who loves me yet;
Who, when the rest shall all forget
    Their rhyming brother,
Will still recall the nights we met,
    And sang together.

Yet kind old Rubbing, bless his heart,
He stood beside me from the start;

Ashes of Roses

He 'll not forget, nor dear old Art,
    He 'll not forget;
He 'll not forget, God bless his heart,
    He 'll not forget.

And what a rare old opportunity
To gas about our great community,
Where mind and man are poised in unity
    To avoid mistakes,
That each, alone, without impunity,
    Forever makes.

I 'd have our vast, extended park,
To ramble in from dawn till dark,
Singing with whip-poor-will or lark,
    As the spirit moved me,
And home again to a Noah's ark
    Of them that loved me.

For I could never live alone,
A hermit king, on any throne;
Give me young children, some my own,
    To romp and meet me;
And a loving wife, a rose full-blown,
    To blush and greet me.

Great artists, too, we 'd have around,
All moods, from simple to profound;
You, Eastie, uppermost and crowned,
    My young heart's friend;

And at your throne of wit, renowned,
    The World would bend.

Afield, the laborers would reign,
The happy kings of toil's domain,
And dress their realms of golden grain,
    Wholesome and scenty,
With peaceful slumber for their pain,
    And smiling plenty.

Sweet wild flowers would blush and blow,
Untouched beneath the genial glow,
That filtered softly down below
    Through cooling bowers,
Or glittered into golden bows
    Through dripping showers.

There, wild, and free, and unbetrayed,
The gentle deer, beneath the shade,
Would crop the tender, dewy blade,
    And mildly stare,
Feeling no cause to be afraid
    Of hunters there.

My nature, constant, unconfined,
Would long, when heavy-souled, to find
A temple, simple, soul-designed,
    Still as the tomb,
Where holy thoughts convey the mind
    Beyond the gloom.

Ashes 'f Roses

When full at heart, alone I'd stray,
Hear music swell and die away,
And feel the echoes sweetly play
        Back in the glow,
And usher out some dying day
        Of long ago.

At harvest even, when all was still,
Hear voices, and far lowing, till
The drowsy air had drunk its fill
        Of gentle sounds,
And daylight slept beyond the hill,
And the low, yellowing moon 'gan swell
        From the wooded grounds.

A mirror lake, in fairy blue,
Winds from my fancy into view;
And far across, it seems that you
        Await the gale,
That soon will start and bring you to,
        With leaning sail.

But circumstances, strange to say,
Don't come around in just that way,
So I must be content to stay
        Here in the city,
And sing my pessimistic lay
        Of scoff and pity.

So, in the midst of city sin,
With Dutch and Dago, French and Finn,

All "rushing growlers" out and in, —
        O Babel nation!
In roar and rumble I begin
        My occupation.

The room I'm writing in is small,
The children talk, and laugh, and squall;
It's home though, — that's the best of all —
        So I don't mind it:
If there's another charm withal,
        I fail to find it.

Four stories up above the ground,
You'd think I couldn't hear a sound;
But I'd be happy if I found
        One lullful minute,
When I might feel a bit profound,
        And make sense in it.

The roar and rumble grinds and grows, —
Car gongs, confusion, — "Po — ta — t-o-e-s!"
The rush of trains, grind organ woes,
        The smell of beer,
Loud-rattling trucks, and "Cash old clothes!
        East! do you hear?

And still the children laugh and sing,
Until I set them ciphering:
They work a while, until they ring
        Their tempers up,

Then, muddle-brained, to me they bring
    Their bitter cup.

They think I'm mean to make them work,
And tell how Alderman O'Rourke
"Allows his Hennessey to shirk
    All he durn pleases,
And lets him play all day in the park,
    Just 'cause he teases."

But soon they laugh at all that's said,
And hit each other on the head,
And yell and screech like fractious dead
    In the devil's pound;
And all because they know I dread
    The slightest sound.

They're children though, and wanton faction
Gives them some empty satisfaction;
And if it drives you to distraction,
    So much more fun:
Just let them see it in your actions,
    And they'll keep on.

Sometimes I sit for hours and pine
About this prosy life of mine,
As if the world were in combine
    Against my pleasure,
Still swearing I can't write a line
    For lack of leisure.

Still, tending to its own affairs,
The busy world ignores my cares,
And friends are busy, too, with theirs,
        And none of mine,
And days pass by me unawares
        Without a line.

Then of a sudden, something said,
Or better, something thought, or read,
Sets me a-going in my head
        Like all creation!
Till I come to again, half dead,
        For more vacation.

And then I mood about my health,
And grumble that I have no wealth
To trans me from these scenes of filth
        Back to the West!
My trunk has dwindled to a twelfth!
        I must have rest!

But when I'm in the rhyming mood,
My poverty, and bachelorhood,
Have no effect for bad or good,
        Unless the latter,
So I won't loiter here to brood
        About the matter.

And why repine, East?   Better times
Are sure to come, when eager dimes

Ashes ʼf Roses

Will answer to my ready rhymes —
      And yet, you know me:
I would not for the pay of crimes
      Set foot below me.

Whatever comes, my will is strong.
I 'll write what suits me, not the throng.
Let days drag hungrier days along
      Into starvation,
I shall not force a single song
      To suit the fashion.

If what contents me please another,
And he would be its foster-father,
To print it, unchanged, altogether,
      As I 'd direct him,
He might imburse me as a brother,
      And I respect him.

Now in this philosophic fit
I quite forgot how much I 've writ;
But I 'll be through now in a bit, —
      Soon as I finish.
(That sounds like good friend Goddard's wit,
      On the diminish.)

But I must twang before I 'm through
The strings I used to twang for you,
And if it drags like Greek review,
      Grin, and forbear me:

I must do what I want to do,
　　　And you must hear me.

Time! I declare! I'm just about
Run down. I never was right stout.
Look at me, East. I have no doubt
　　　I've grown much thinner.
I must be sick. I'm all played out.
　　　I — I smell my dinner.

Good-bye! Good-bye! You hear me sobbing?
My love to Josh and dear old Rubbing,
Broad-breasted-brother-Bruce a clubbing,
　　　Bless his stretched hide,
And — there! — I feel a kind of throbbing
　　　In my inside!

ANOTHER TO EASTIE.

Hello Old East! I span the pen
To scribble you some lines again,
Though up to date I've no such den
　　　To warm my zeal,
As I've enlarged on now and then
　　　As my ideal.

Imagine, now, we're out at sea,
The natural place for you and me,

Ashes of Roses

And let our destination be
    New York, whimback,
As strangers, how impatiently
    We pace the deck.

For we have read so much concerning
The city's culture, art, and learning,
That we 've looked on to our sojourning
    For some years past:
And now we rise the morrow morning
    To live at last.

At early morning, o'er the rail
We lean and watch each gleaming sail,
And drink the freshness from the gale
    With eager lips,
Or wave our handkerchiefs to hail
    The passing ships.

At evening now the unclean gale
Blows round the sun a murky veil;
While many a dark and smoky sail
    Glides slowly by,
And distant steamboats moan and wail
    Along the sky.

Now through the Narrows, past the forts,
And in the great bay, lined with ports,
Where craft of many shapes and sorts,
    With solemn speed,

Move swiftly toward each other's thwarts,
  Yet never heed.

Look where the hill divides in two,
And shows the darkening ocean through.
See sails cheer up the gloomy blue,
  Far, far away.
Here, lingering, whisper to the view,
  "Farewell, O sea!"

"Farewell; but soon shall we return,
When trifling pleasures sickening turn,
And all our heavy souls shall yearn
  To be with thee;
To see, and hear, and love to learn
  Thy charms, O sea!"

While still across the rail we lean,
In deep communion with the scene,
The dark hills slowly intervene;
  And still the sea
Is breaking, breaking, all unseen,
  'Round you and me.

Still where the red sun closed his eye,
And streaked along the glowing sky,
The dark clouds catch the rays that fly
  Till all are gone;
And now they watch the daylight die,
  And night come on.

Ashes of Roses

As twilight fades and dies away,
The pale moon brightens in the bay,
While twinkling stars come out to play
      In the chill night air,
And lights come shimmering on their way
      From everywhere.

See lining all the dark'ning shore,
Great ships of commerce, state, and war,
Whose thousand naked masts implore,
      With outstretched arms,
To join the moonlit clouds that soar
      Beyond the storms.

And farther back, confused and dense,
Dark buildings, squatty or immense,
Rear like a giant's mouldering fence
      Against the sky ;
And on where deeper glooms commence,
      They blur and die.

Silent, conspicuous, and grand,
Like some ship from a holy land,
Moved swiftly by an unseen hand,
      A steamboat, white,
Heads seaward from the darkened land,
      Out in the night.

And now a tug with noise and grind,
Its black smoke puffing in the wind,

Its train of garbage boats behind,
    Steams out to sea.
Crime, fleeing from the enlightened mind
    Of times to be.

Now naked ships, now wharves are passed;
On one of these our ropes are cast;
And when the vessel's good and fast,
    We go ashore:
Our trip is done—New York at last—
    The sea no more.

Day after day the motley crowd,
Tobacco-mouthed and trouble-bowed,
The heartless rich, the poor and proud,
    In open fight,
Win what they can, foul means allowed,
    If hid from sight.

The unknown great, the over-rated,
The groveller, and the elevated,
The sterling worth, the showy plated,
    Healthy or shattered,
Like grain and chaff unseparated,
    By Fortune scattered.

Just watch them as they hurry by,
With hollow, dissipated eye,
The smart, the dull, the mean, the sly,
    Children and sires,

Ashes of Roses

All rushing on to gratify
       To-night's desires.

And many a bar-sponge, soaked and fed,
The fat rolls creased beneath his head,
His belly like an annexed shed,
       Securely hung,
His legs from interference spread,
       Waddles along.

Year after year they flood their sewers,
Until they bloat like German brewers;
And still the sloppy liquor lures,
       And still they follow,
Till, human hogs, no pride endures,
       And low they wallow.

Along the streets you see the fruits
In homeless, blank-eyed, staggering brutes,
Gangrened and rotten to the roots
       With drink and crime,
Each a sad cancer that pollutes
       The face of Time.

Sometimes, with stumbling steps careered,
A drunken she, bloat-faced and bleared,
Her rags with gutter-mud besmeared,
       Her face with gleet,
By neither sense nor instinct steered,
       Moves down the street.

Hooting and jeering for the devil's sake,
Buckets in hand, the hoodlums take
Their noisy way along the wake
      Of human sinning,
Nor aught ashamed that there they make
      Their young beginning.

The sight of "cops" will still the noise,
And awe, but not dispel the boys,
Who wait until the big convoys
      Move with their show,
Then follow in the keenest joys
      That hoodlums know.

But not each boy who thus behaves,
Will end his life with bawds and knaves,
For human honor oftener saves
      Than crime is taught,
But such scenes are the early graves
      Of manly thought.

And children, raised as most are here,
Where right and wrong are never clear,
And reputation none too dear,
      Soon go astray.
Used to its sights, they seldom fear
      The downward way.

The dissipated crowd at nights,
Parading in the glaring lights,

Ashes of Roses

To me the saddest of street sights,
        Draws no attention.
So common are the loose delights,
        Few dare to mention.

There, brazen in the lewd parade,
The wanton, once a little maid,
Still young, perhaps, but soon to fade,
        Refall, corrode,
Walks shameless with some renegade
        To Sin's abode.

Still, girls of every age and size
Run on the streets, and compromise
What modesty we may surmise
        Was theirs by birth.
How many, think you, ever rise
        To any worth?

And mothers, degenerate in their tastes,
Prefer the gratitude of beasts,
And all their sick affections waste
        In poodle kissing.
And lively children, once displaced,
        Are always missing.

Whatever window —and they're few—
I'm writing near, and looking through,
A brick wall flattens on my view
        Across the way,

Ashes of Roses

Of patch design, but "Something new,"
    The owners say.

Most architects here vaguely clutch
At any symbol, Greek or Dutch,
Which, made of tin, won't cost too much,
    But, boldly placed,
Will show some master's able touch,
    And owner's taste.

Old mansions, crumbling to decay,
Tell of good taste long passed away.
Some, new, foretell that better day
    We long to see,
When wealth will cease to buy display,
    Or cease to be.

Some show with narrow fronts erect,
How painfully the architect
Designed to draw some good effect
    Out of distortion;
And here and there you may detect
    Some pleasing portion.

Fantastic office towers rise
To giddy heights up through the skies,
All craning for the greatest size
    At the smallest cost,
Till ancient, simple Beauty flies,
    And art is lost.

Ashes of Roses

Monotonously vulgar styles
Flank the loud streets in rigid piles,
Blocks upon blocks, miles upon miles,
    League after league,
Long, dim, reverberating aisles,
    Thronged with fatigue.

No native workman drives the nail,
And sings along the scaffold rail,
Or stops to give that hearty hail
    We love to hear;
But low-browed Latins rush the pail,
    And swig their beer.

And ah, they find no flowery homes;
But vaulted streets of catacombs,
Where poor like rats, and rich like gnomes,
    Sleep when they must,
Stifled in close, gas-lighted tombs
    Of noise and dust.

The poor, where churches rise in gloom,
Read "Welcome."—Yes, to standing room;
For shabby folk should not presume
    To sit in pews:
They're for the rich, who can assume
    The heavy dues.

The standard being flash and cash,
The shabby poor are counted trash;

Ashes of Roses

So all aspire to "cut a dash,"
    Ev'n though they rue it,
And live on counter lunch and hash
    So they can do it.

Most people live here but to show
How rich they are, how much they know,
And each thing bought must help to throw
    The light desired;
And when they get it, out they go
    To be admired.

This wealth, to which they all aspire,
Fans at the flames of hot desire,
Consumes their virtues in the fire,
    And steels their hearts,
Till they love none, and none admire
    Their soulless parts.

Here you may see the grizzly tramp,
With red face like a danger lamp,
His matted whiskers hanging damp
    With drying beer:
And here you see grim Hunger's cramp,
    And Sorrow's tear.

Here loll in cabs the pampered wealth;
There families breathe the fumes of filth;
While dread Disease steals on with stealth
    And saps them both,

Ashes of Roses

To make room for another tilth
    Of ranker growth.

There is a great deal more to say
Of jewelled rich in swell array,
Contrasted with their brother clay,—
    Of parks, and drives,
Where people rest, and children play,
    And health survives.

The poor man takes his children there
To breathe the pleasant woodland air,—
The only profit he may share
    With outraged pride,
Who, in hot summer, live somewhere
    By the seaside.

Poor little children, helpless, weak,—
Oh Eastie, how can I be meek,
When from their eyes the hollows speak,
    "Blessed are we,"
And sunken chest and hungry cheek,
    "Come unto me."

Ah, why will men flock to the city,
Where Sin is sought, and Filth is witty,
And Truth will shock them without pity,
    If they be pure,
And they themselves grow harsh and gritty
    Beyond endure.

New York! bar-room of dissipation!
Ball-room of frenzied fascination!
Eyesore and glory of the nation!
With all thy blots,—
From all thy beastly degradation
Are spared some spots.

Oh for the fields! the lanes! the sky!
With fleets of cloud-ships sailing by,—
To be a bird! and fly, and fly,
O'er lake and river,
Away, away, until I die!
And on forever.

STANZAS OF A COMMUNION.

Almighty God, in gratitude I come,
Though frail of thought, and dumb,
Craving that mercy shown
Through all these years when I have walked alone.
Though long ungrateful, now before Thy throne,
Such gratitude I own,
As only Thou, O God, can understand.
Take Thou my erring hand
And lead me to the light when darkness gathers 'round
the land.

Thou knowest the difference between life and creed.
Doctrine is but a weed,
That winds itself among

The strings of reason, delicately strung.
Thou knowest their discord with my pen and tongue
In all the songs I 've sung.
But now my faith is in the coming years ;
And gladly, without tears,
I bid farewell to gloomy creeds that justified my fears.

Why did I stay to reason with mute Fate,
Till fears, fast growing great,
First darkened hope, then faith?
I found me on my way to meet sad Death,
With power, but little will, to draw the breath
I scarce preferred to death.
But now my faith is in the coming years,
When kindness, and not jeers,
Shall wean us from the subtle creeds that designate
        God's heirs.

Not through these tedious years have I alone
Stood pondering at Thy throne;
Nor in the growing gloom
That fast devoured the darkness of my doom
Have I alone longed for some hope to loom
Out of my dead hope's tomb.
But now my faith is in the coming years;
The glad, millennial years ;
When men shall see how wrong it was to circumscribe
        their prayers.

Why will men tell me I am cursed with doubt?
Though thousands figure out

That Thou art less than Thine,
Crowds cannot make fictitious wrath divine.
Thou art still God ; and no man should assign
Thy limits, Lord, nor mine.
Let me have patience.   In the coming years
The darkness disappears.
And they who live in those great days shall not be
    vexed with fears.

Blessed are they who never question why,
But hope that by and by,
When their hard day is done,
And they lie down in peace at set of sun,
On the bright morrow they shall meet with one
They loved, but who is gone.
For ah, they know that in the coming years
There shall be no more tears,
And they shall see Thy kind, sweet face, and Thy
    home shall be theirs.

Then let me not in vain conceit presume
To reason out my doom,
More than to idly scan
The thousand different destinies of man ;
For since the course of time with Thee began,
Thou hast obscured Thy plan,
That we might live in hope, and humbly share,
Each as his strength can bear,
The burden of misfortune with the least of its
    despair.

So is my lot the lot of all mankind.
And we, though future-blind,
Paint pictures of the day
It pleases us to feel not far away.
So let me live that while I watch and pray,
I cheer the long delay;
And should joy never come to me below,
Give me Thy peace to know
That in the Great Hereafter I shall find it where I go.

Thou knowest it all; Oh why should I rehearse
Thus, in my humble verse,
Thy goodness, gracious Lord?
For not in my poor language is the word
That can express to Thee what Thou hast heard
Deep in my silence stirred.
Thou knowest my feelings best, for Thou dost bring
This very song I sing
Out of the fullness of my soul, Oh Thou my Lord, my
        King.

So I commit my future life to Thee;
And though I cannot see,
Yet will I always trust
That Thou wilt lead me where Thou thinkest just.
And when at last I leave here, as I must,
May men revere my dust,
And speak with charity of him whose days,
Though spent in these strange ways,
Yet grew a blessing to the world because he sang Thy
        praise.

A LITTLE BIRD.

Poor little eyes, look not so scared,
I'm not the fiend that peeped and glared
Along the sights as he prepared
      To end thy song.
He shall not come now, little bird,
      To do thee farther wrong.

Down where the trees stand gold and gray
Against the lingering grief of day,
He takes his gun and sneaks away
      Into the woods,
Like some scared thief who dares not stay
      To claim his goods.

There, there, I know pain racks thy breast,
And Death knocks hard to be thy guest,
But soon shall come a happier rest
      On some sweet shore,
Where beasts, nor men, nor Death molest
      Forevermore.

There, it is over; seek thy home.
Go, blameless spirit of the dumb.
And I shall hear thee when I come,
      And thou shalt know
That he who ached to help thee some
      Was not thy foe.

And so I place thee in the ground,
Where thy poor, bleeding form I found,

And build o'er thee a little mound
Of silent clay,
And plant some drooping flowers around,
And go away.

Oh Thou Who gave the little birds,
Whose songs are sweeter than our words,
Teach me such humble, simple chords
Of modest thought,
That in the lessons life affords
I learn all that I ought.

"IN THE HOLLOW OF HIS HAND."

Here let me linger by the wild seashore,
Alone with Thee, to Whom the mighty roar
Sounded Thy praises through the ages past,
Proclaims them still, and will proclaim at last.
Now, at Thy mute, unquestionable will,
The deep gloom gathers, and the winds are still;
And all the fearful energies of space
Draw up their chariots for the mighty race.
Silent they roll along the scowling heaven:
Now breathless wait till Thy command be given.
The frightened sea-birds, screaming up the bay,
Seek shelter where their echoes died away.
Still, wide-expanding, rolls the mighty sea,
Its thousand voices still proclaiming Thee.
Hushed is the world,—now balmy breezes blow,
Faintly at first, but gathering as they go.

A distant rumbling, awful and profound,
Dies far away, and stills the world around.
Now while the last reverberations die
Along the vaulted windows of the sky,
The heavens crack! forth from the fissures fly
Illumined streaks, and kindle all the sky!
The winds increase. With every flaming lance
The heavens rattle and the glooms advance.
Faster and faster down the quaking course
The tempests thunder with increasing force.
Louder and louder roar the foaming waves,
The lightning flashes and the tumult raves.
Now torrents deluge all the flooded scene,
And deep the muffled thunder rolls between.
Across the ravaged land the lightnings spread,
Trees stand an instant, and again are hid.
The rain, deserting, follows with the wind:
It hurries on and leaves the flood behind;
Yet still it sprinkles, slower still, and slow,
And swollen torrents seek the sea below;
While puffing winds, all out of breath, appear,
With clouds and sunshine bringing up the rear.

NEW YORK AND THE HUDSON.

Hail! mighty Tomb, once more dull morning breaks
    Upon the stupor of a million souls.
Ah, lonely city, my impatience aches
    To run from thee beyond the farthest poles.
My footsteps echo down thy stony streets,

"Farewell, farewell," they say, and my heart beats.
Hail! mighty River. Lo, from where I stand,
 On the high point of thy proud Palisades,
I see thy winding bosom, still and grand,
 Flow far away in morning mists and shades;
Where quiet distance dreams in purple glades,
 And spirit sails suggest that ever on
The world grows brighter as the future fades.
 Farewell, no charms can hold me,—I am gone

FROM THE SPANISH.

I.

And then there appeared in her eyes a tear,
 At my lips a phrase of pardon.
But her eyes were dried by cruel Pride,
 And my lips still held their burden.

I go my way, she hers.
 But love is long and deep.
"Oh why," I say, "did I pause that day?"
And she, "Why did I not weep?"

II.

For a look, a world.
 For a smile, a heaven.
For a kiss, I know not what,
 But were it mine, 'twere given.

III.

Sighs return to the air and are not.
Back to the sea the salt tears flow.
But tell me, woman, when love is forgot,
Where does it go?

ART AND NATURE.

Unnerved one day, and sad and sick at heart,
I snatched my hat and sought the open air.
In vain I'd racked the last resource of art
To tell in verse the depth of some despair;
Swiftly I walked, I cared not why nor where;
And as I went, tore in a thousand bits
The worthless remnant of the rhymed affair
That cost my nerves, and overtaxed my wits.
"Ah me," I thought, "where are the benefits?"
The sun went down.   The stars in silence came,
And looked at me; and it was dark and still.
I could just see the delicate, slender flame
Of the new moon, retiring o'er the hill.
I thought of God; and all was dark and still.

COMMUNIONS.

I.

Thou Who canst make me what I most would be,
I love to consecrate my lines to Thee,

I love to praise Thee,—Oh, to sing Thy praise
In worthy manhood, and in gentle ways,
Be half my life;—the other half to do
The greatest good that Thou shalt turn me to.
Though cold the crowd, and hard to entertain,
The good may hear, the wise will not complain.
There waits some sympathy for every cause,
Most for the just, who work without applause.

II.

Almighty God, Thou glorious King of kings,
Eternal Ruler of unnumbered worlds,
That through vast ages in yon pathless heaven
Pursue their awful course in harmony!
Oh wondrous Being, God of every race,
To whom a million souls this moment look
With sweet, confiding hope,—look Thou on me.
Stretch forth Thy hand, Oh God of love, and here,
While evening shades prevail, and deeper gloom
Steals on the world, speak to my waiting soul.

He Who provides for little birds,
    And gives them tongues to sing,
Who spreads the grass for helpless herds,
    And shades the cooling spring,
He in His love will not forget
    His children must be fed,
And when our board with thanks is set,
    Will grant our daily bread.

Ashes of Roses

MY MOTHER.

Child of the wind, I passed my early days
In solitary strolls and sweet content.
Well known to me were all sequestered ways,
Where I might go and not feel indolent.
The world was new, and all its wide extent
An open book, whose leaves were ever turning.
· The more I saw, the farther on I went,
Till, vexed with thoughts and premature discerning,
Content gave way too soon to strong desire for learning.

Brooks learned to know me, and the modest flowers
Hid in the grass as I passed their habitude.
And in green thickets, cool with secret bowers,
I crept and watched the catbird's hungry brood.
And oft in depths of woodland solitude,
Where towered the trees like giants o'er my head,
I stopped and listened, fearful to intrude
On the hushed slumbers of the ancient dead,
Of whose wild deeds and myths I, like a boy, had read.

Out nutting all alone I sometimes heard
Quick rustling in the autumn leaves around,
Caused by some busy squirrel, or songless bird,
Or frost-bit nut in dropping to the ground.
Instinctively I turned whence came the sound,
And something moved behind me — two — and three,
Until I shuddered, and looked all around,
Expecting something from behind each tree
To peep with grinning face, and poke sly fun at me.

Ashes o' Roses

I dreamed of greatness; and each next success
Lifted me up, and set my aim the higher.
I schooled, reschooled, but in the practic mess
Lost time, and poise, and half my former fire.
My teachers taught me I must not aspire,
But dig, that I might some day earn, and make.
Who, when I left their deep scholastic mire,
To sing and study for pure pleasure's sake,
Misunderstood me for a worthless rhyming rake.

There comes a time when we must lose our friends,
Or try their friendship; and when I was grown
Vexed with advice that ridiculed my ends,
I left their ruts for highways of my own.
One withering flower I loved, but she was gone.
She who was always patient, even with me.
My mother, oh my mother,—how alone—
How sad and lonely when I long for thee,
And think of all the weary years that yet must be.

I had a dream last night, and even now
My mind refuses to be reconciled.
'T is so confused, I cannot tell just how,
But seems I was at first a little child.
The day was just like this—so calm and mild
It seemed some special blessing in the land.
My mother came and kissed me, and she smiled
As on we walked together, hand in hand,
And spake no words, yet seemed to understand.

She led me on, and when there came sharp stones
Took me in arms, but seemed to walk with pain;

For in her breast I felt the stifled groans,
Until she stood me in the clear again.
And then we came where trees were dark with rain,
And seemed to me I'd been that way before.
But long before the day began to wane
My little feet were very tired and sore,
And so she took me in her arms once more.

The grumbling sky grew black, and frightful forms
Loomed in the lightning flashes, and were gone.
They seize my head and hurl me through the storms;
And round I whirl through space, and on, and on—
Stop—stop me—O—! Still rolling on, and on,
Past clanging spheres and worlds of wild-eyed dead,
Till, black as death, eternal midnights yawn—
I plunge—I strike—: beside my whirling bed
My mother, leaning, soothes my fevered head.

I must have fallen asleep once more, and dreamed;
For still I heard the rolling worlds and stars,
Still growing fainter in my ears, it seemed,
Like midnight rushing of the distant cars;
Now singing like a thousand soft guitars,
Faint, and more faint, till far away, methought,
I heard the tinkling of the tiny stars,
That danced in dazzling millions as they wrought,
Through ringing stillness, those faint sounds I caught.

And then it seemed I heard my mother sing,
Like some sweet angel voice, and far away,
About the little bird that came in Spring,

And sang so sweetly at the dawn of day.
And when the last sad accents died, I lay
Weeping, to think my little bird had flown.
Again that voice from Heaven seemed to say:
"Poor mamma's little bird will soon be grown,
To fly away, and leave her all alone."

We stood indoors and watched the busy rain,—
I and my sister and our baby brother.
It crept so sadly down the window pane,
That as in love we drew us close together,
And put our little arms round one another,
My sister leaned her head on mine and wept.
And then a door was opened, and my mother
Lay in a dark sick-room where watch was kept;
And solemn women whispered that she slept.

This changed; and the scared darkness seemed to
        cower
Behind the black, wet trees that dripped between,
And the warm sun burst through the misty shower,
That fell like spray upon the sparkling scene.
Another shift: no windows intervene,
And it was later morning, and so bright
That little birds chirped loudly from the green,
And butterflies were fluttering in the light.
They flew, I flew, time flew, and it was night.

And winding paths turned off in all directions.
Some disappeared in scrambling crowds and mire,

And some seemed lost in misty recollections,
That passed them by on grounds but little higher ;
Where loomed dim shapes of consequences dire,
That beckoned me to follow, and then hid,
And peeped so at me with their eyes of fire
That though I felt my inner voice forbid,
I stepped the slippery path, and would have slid.

Then supperless to bed ; but not to sleeping ;
For soon that well-known footstep on the stair :
My mother came, her sweet face wet with weeping,
And spread her bounty on the bedroom chair.
Ah, many a time I ate my supper there,
And told of all the wondrous things I 'd seen,
Exaggerating how, and when, and where,
With all the license of a bard serene,
And bites and swallows choked like interludes
        between.

Her grateful eyes no more shall meet my own
With glad approval and maternal pride.
Through weary life I take my way alone,
And try so hard to feel well satisfied ;
But life is oh so long, the world so wide,
That though in dreams I see her o'er and o'er,
When shall I turn me from life's sad seaside,
And meet my mother on that farther shore,
Where I may be with her, at rest forevermore.

THE DEGENERATE.

They 's no use a-talkin', us Hoosiers is green.
  What we lack is the citified knack
Of bein' real wicked without bein' mean.
  I jack! I know fer a fac'.
Ef you 'd only a-saw all the doins' I seen
At the opries, et cetery, you 'd ketch whut I mean.
An' fellers, I swan! ef my pile wuzn't lean,
  By crack! I'd wanto go back.

The wimmun wuz rigged jest to worry the min.
  My—oh! but wuzn't they though!
With their fancy silk corsets an' perty white skin,
  Jest as low as they dast fer to show.
Did I look? Course I looked. Turn your head ef you
    kin,
Shet your eyes an' cote Scripcher, an' say it 's a sin,
But the first thing you know you 're a-lookin' agin.
  Can't go agin natcher you know.

I seen Thingabobski, too, one night—
  I sware! you 'd ort-a-ben there.
Folks says he 's a wonder, but that ain't quite
  No-where near to compare.
I wouldn't a-minded his playin' a mite,
But I see right away the man wuzn't right;—
Why I never in all my life see sech a sight—
  I dee-clare! he wuz' nuthin' but hair.

The people clapped hands an' waited a bit,
  An' a whole gang got up an' sang.

An' then this hyere feller fell into a fit. —
  Gee—whang—lippitty—bang!
Folks got so excited they couldn't sit;
An' I got up, an' ef I didn't git!
An' I'll bet you that idjut's a-goin' it yit
  With his gol-dang pi-anner herangue.

It strikes me these musical folks, as a rule,
  Takin' 'um jes' as they come
The whole world over, is mostly a fool,—
  Clean plum daffy, I gum.
Putt a hairy I-talyern on a pi-anner stool
To playin' them toons they call icicle school,
An' they rolls their eyes round like a sun-struck
    mule.
  An' yit some can't fiddle ner drum.

AN APPEAL FOR THE ARMENIANS.

Long I've looked in trust to England to espouse the
    Christian cause,
Vainly hopeful of the time to sing her well-deserved
    applause.
All the world has watched and waited.   Christendom
    has hoped in vain.
Still the daily news of slaughter swells the number of
    the slain.
Every day a band of martyrs from an old and honored
    race;

Every day before all Europe grows the mountain of
    disgrace.
Fifty thousand helpless Christians slain by order of one
    man,
For they chose the Holy Bible to the blood-stained
    Alkoran.
Thousands, suffering from starvation, shiver round the
    crowded fire,
Silent, watchful every minute, lest they wake the
    sultan's ire;
While the generous Western World outside stands
    knocking at the door,
With a wealth of food and clothing in her ships along
    the shore.
But their king refuses entrance as he wipes the bloody
    knife,
And, before her dying parents, gives the little child
    to wife.
And he laughs in cold derision at the pleadings of the
    world,
Where the jealousy of nations keeps the flags of battle
    furled.
For the tyrant of the many wives enjoys the sounds
    he hears,
Glad to gratify his lusts, and proud to move the world
    to tears.

Oh thou patient, blameless people, many a heart this
    side the sea
Rises from the daily pulse to beat in sympathy with
    thee.

Ashes of Roses

Many a husband feels the anguish, many a mother
    holds her breath,
Reading of thy wives and daughters forced to horrors
    worse than death.
And they see thy sacred homes to dens of violation
    turned,
Where the shrines of thy devoted love are shamed to
    death, and burned.
While around thee crowd the nations, big with dignity
    of state,
Striving with a heathen monarch for the honors of
    debate.
Jealous, watchful of each other, see them bow and
    scrape with care:
Fearful of the secret dagger; quick to use it when
    they dare.
Verged on righteous war they argue, till they force
    him to explain,
When, their mission half accomplished, see them strut
    back home again.
They would help thee, so they tell us, but none dares
    when all object;
And thy pleadings for protection but insure thee their
    neglect.
So they leave thee with his promise; but no sooner
    are they gone,
Than he pays thy persecutors, and the bloody work
    goes on.
Helpless in the hands of heathen; left by Christians
    to thy cares;
For diplomacy itself has failed, and 'tis no fault of
    theirs.

Friends of such, whate'er your station, God shall
    some day try your creed,
And your self-control shall choke you when your
    heart comes home to bleed.
You shall reason to your own content when He shall
    ask you why,
In the ready hour of action, you were waiting idly
    by.
Would you, if you saw a man assault your wife, or
    kill your cat,
Pause in both alike to argue, like a well-bred
    diplomat?
Would you then, for sake of friendship with the mighty
    man you fear,
Make a virtue of your patience, and pretend you did
    not hear?
Who shall dare be diplomatic when a woman cries for
    help,
Shall be scorned of men forever, lower than the lowest
    whelp:
Doomed by Truth to shame eternal, he shall shine
    with bloody Turks,
Where the blackest page in history holds his diplo-
    matic works.

Shame, oh shame, ye powers of Europe, on your
    hypocritic state!
You have homage for the mighty; for the weak you
    have but hate;
Yet you call your countries Christian, fighting for the
    Martyr's cross:

Boil you down to Christ's religion, and behold the
    princely dross.
Are you civilized as nations? do you show it in your
    deeds,
While you watch your brothers butchered by these
    systematic breeds?
What the use of modern warfare, power and pride of
    kings' command,
When full fifty thousand Christians perish by a single
    hand?
Where that old and mighty nation now, that boasts a
    power supreme?
Is adoption of the helpless not an item of her scheme?
No, alas, the poor Armenians have no wealth of daz-
    zling store,
To effect that strange decorum, sold so many times
    before.
Theirs is not the rich East Indies, tempting to the
    British greed;
If it were, some page in history long had held a
    British deed.
Theirs no wealth of minor countries, to be watched as
    soon as found;
If it were, long years of mortgage now had Anglicized
    the ground.
Theirs no mines of Venezuela, hardly known to local
    fame,
Ere the bafflers of the sunset move their boundary line
    to claim;
Where, no sooner other mines are found beyond the
    bounding hill,

Than the all-begrudging nation moves her limits
     farther still.
Then she fights if necessary, but in cases like this
     one,
Stops at show of stately wisdom, and declares her
     duty done.
From the taking of her island, to the charging of the
     Boer,
This, the mightiest state in history, never fought a
     righteous war;
Where the right was half the battle, and a trust in
     God the rest,
And they won, none could remember how, but God
     knew what was best.
Oh thou proud and boastful people, vain of e'en thine
     empty pride ;
Self-made lords of half the world, and coveters of all
     beside;
You who place the heads of families, unimproved from
     age to age,
O'er the freedom of your manhood, to be heard above
     the sage:
You, to whom had been the glory, now to you the
     just disgrace ;
You who had the power to save them, turn, oh turn
     and hide your face.
You will force the honest settler from the home himself
     has made,
But you dare not help a people with their monarch's
     debts unpaid.

Would to God some manly feeling stirred a statesman,
 or a king,
Who, despite the threats of Russia, dares to do the
 manly thing!
Why should Russia, more than Turkey—any half-bar-
 baric state—
In the face of such as England still control Armenia's
 fate?
Is her brutal exile system too monotonous to bear,
That she joins her force with Turkey for a new enjoy-
 ment there?
He who holds in trust the power, and permits this
 shameful work,
Will be held to task through centuries for a coward,
 and a shirk.
For the God who strives to teach us by the task that
 must be done,
Sends the man ordained to do it, as He sent His mar-
 tyred Son;
As He sent our country's father to reward our
 righteousness,
Lincoln in the time of trouble, Hamilton in time of
 peace.
He, the lofty man of genius who shall rise above the
 clod
And perform the will of Heaven, shall be deemed a
 son of God.—
Shall be looked upon as a chosen for the duties of the
 day,
And his name be held in reverence when his soul has
 passed away.

Oh whoe'er ye be that hear Him, whether high in
    power or no ;
Ye who from the thrones of Europe view the modest
    world below ;
Ye who feel the man within you struggling to assert
    the right :
Marshal on the plains of justice, and in name of God
    unite !
With one motive fixed in Heaven, that forgets all
    private gain,
Let us do His will Who sent us, that He send us not
    in vain.

Ye who, great in power by nature, occupy our seats
    of state,
Show us why we sent you thither ; cease, oh cease the
    long debate.
Every boy we send to college learns to use the pom-
    pous phrase :
Not to such, but men of action, comes the everlasting
    praise.
You have feebly recommended, in such tones as none
    will heed,
That they take decisive action, when they 're ready to
    proceed ;
But is that the tone for freemen, who, a month or two
    ago,
Sided with a weaker country, and declared the strong
    their foe?
Oh my people, friends of freedom, can we not by
    strength of voice

Shame the cowardice of England till her conscience
    leaves no choice?
Till she must neglect her interests, and remembering
    God's alone,
In the face of all the Russians hurl the tyrant from
    the throne?
Can we not, oh ye my people, if she choose the
    righteous course,
Offer in God's name to help her to the limit of our force?
Oh consider but the helpless, what delay to them must
    cost.
If we shed our blood to help them, surely more is
    gained than lost.
There is room for bolder action ere we reach the end
    of sense,
And the powers will have to hear us when we leave
    them no defense.
If you argue, use expressions that convey the thoughts
    you mean ;
Not expand yourselves in pompous clause, with cour-
    tesies between.
You may yet redeem your standing in the sight of God
    and man,
But the weeks are lost in talking, and 'tis time the
    work began.
May be at this very moment, while we speak the
    awful words,
Some one sees his helpless sweetheart ravished by the
    heartless Kurds:
Fiercely now he draws to help her, struggling, calling
    on her name :—

Bound, Oh God! secure and helpless, he must see her
    forced to shame!
Grind his teeth in frantic frenzy as he hurls the spiteful
    curse!
But the rising flames of passion but consume his soul
    the worse.
Prone he falls upon his temples; digs his fingers in his
    flesh;
Cries aloud to Christ for mercy, tearing wildly at the
    lash;
And the boiling blood to issue from each hot and
    swollen vein,
Rushes throbbing through the channels to the flood-
    gates of his brain;
Where the tumult of his being is the only sound he
    hears,
Like the noisy winds of heaven rushing through his
    empty ears.
Round and round his bulging eyeballs wildly swims
    the sick'ning sight;
Fainter grow the nerve convulsions; darker, darker
    grows the night:
Quick the sound of loud explosion runs a quiver
    through his frame,
And he gasps for breath to answer as he hears her call
    his name.
But the heavy world is sinking through the awful
    depths of space;
And he feels the light of Heaven shining on his up-
    turned face;

Sees the gates of Heaven open; hears the angel voices
    ring,—
Lo, the hallowed band of martyrs, Christ Himself, and
    God the King!
And he takes his place among them, with his loved
    ones by his side,
Where, in robes of simple whiteness, shines his pure
    and spotless bride.
Vacant places wait around him for the martyrs that
    shall fall,—
Far beneath, in outer darkness, burns the writing on
    the wall.
Slowly fades the scene beneath him, like a dream of
    long ago,
And he sees the peaceful Jordan, where the flowers
    eternal grow.
Softly now the sounds of music, wafted from celestial
    choirs,
Wander through the hush of Heaven, with the swells
    of golden lyres;
And the bliss of life eternal, where all sorrows pass
    away,
Has absorbed the past and future in one everlasting
    day.

God protect the poor Armenians, if my hurried song
    shall fail
To arouse one friend of freedom on the bloody Turkish
    trail.
Oh that still among our people were the bards of yes-
    terday,

Who, like golden rays at evening, faded from the
    night away.
How might they, in mighty chorus, sing the battle-
    songs of right,
Call their fellow-men together, and inspire their souls
    with might!
And if still there lives a poet, who aspires to honest
    fame,
Let him sing what I 've attempted; let the world
    revere his name.
And where'er he leads his people in the cause of God
    and man,
He who sings this song shall follow, though he do but
    what he can.

A PLOWBOY LULLABY.

My little plowboy is tired to-night,
    And he nods in his high-chair so,
That he must have finished his appetite,
All ready to go to the land of light,
    Where the sleepy plowboys go.

Then come with father, the big plow-man,
    And we 'll sit in the twilight gray,
While our dear little mother, as fast as she can,
    Is clearing the supper away.
And she 'll come too, when her work is through,
    For a shepherdess, I am told,

Finds the little sheep that have fallen asleep,
And carries them into the fold.

Slowly the light fades out of the west,
  Where the long, dark furrows run,
And each little cloud is a floating nest,
Moving too slowly to follow the rest,
  That follow the golden sun.

Then come with father, the big plow-man,
  Till he puts your nightie on,—
But we'll have to be as quick as we can,
  Or the nests will all be gone;
And then wouldn't it be too bad, you see,
  To be left behind to-night,
And miss a day of such pleasant play
  In the beautiful land of light.

See where the first star blinks and peeps
  Over the orchard hill.
All through the long, dark night he keeps
His silent watch, while the great world sleeps,
  And the farmer's voice is still.

But far in the land of light, they say,
  The stars are so near the ground,
You can see all the plowing as plain as day
  For miles and miles around.
For they plow all night in the land of light,
  In the fields of blue and gold,

And the furrows run to the rising sun
　　As they did in the days of old.

Hark ! how the early robin sings
　　Her last good-night to thee ;
And dreams of the tiny pairs of wings,
And the mouths of her featherless little things,
And all the joys that summer brings,
　　And her mate that is to be.

So my little plowboy drifts afloat
　　In the tiny cloud that waits
In the failing light, like a golden boat,
　　Over the pasture gates.
Darker, and darker they seem to grow,
　　Till they anchor one by one,
Under the lee of the slumber sea ;
　　And the voyage of day is done.

NEXT DAY.

Ever'body 'cep' but Ed
Ain't got up yet out a-bed.
We 're nain't goin' to have no more
Picnics, 'cause my papa 's sore.
An' bofe ar brovers groans an' groans,
Nen turns over iss like stones
In neir beds, an' ast me please
Won't I bring nat yeller grease

To 'um, what my mamma rubs
On my toes when neir been stubs.
Nen I bring it, an' ney 're says
"You 're ne bullies' boy ney is."

LITTLE EDGAR.

"Noisy little Edgar,
  Come to me," I said,—
"Don't you know that Reuben
  Is very sick a-bed?
Don't you know, my little man,
  That when you walk about
You should go very slow,
Softly, softly on tip-toe,
  Going in and out?"

Generous little Edgar,
  He did just as I said:
He tip-toed there where Reuben
  Was lying sick in bed,
And round the room, and back again,
  Seriously all about,
Very slow, to and fro,
Softly, softly on tip-toe,
  Out and in and out.

Gentle little Edgar.
  When mamma spoke he said:

78

"Sh—!" and raised his finger,
  And shook his little head,
And peeped out doors where Effie was,
  And whispered all about
How to go to and fro,
Softly, softly on tip-toe,
  Going in and out.

" Precious little Edgar,
  Come to me," I said,
And patient Reuben laughed so hard
  He fairly shook the bed.
"Don't you know, my little man,
  That isn't what I meant?
Run away now and play,—
You will understand some day."
  And away he went.

CONCERNING FACES, SNOOTS, ETC.

Yes an' if you're make a face,
  Er make a snoot, er swear,—
Iss at home er nany place,
  Don't make no differnce where,—
Er holler "Hey!" er stick your tongue
Out at folks 'at goes along,
My mamma says first thing you know
The p'leece'll come, an' off you're 'll go
    Skrait to ne station-house
    In ne control wagon.

WINTER.

Watch out dah, fu' we's a-comin'!
　　Grab on tight an' hol' yo' bref!
D' ain't no one kin tell what happm
　　Ef she tu'n to right o' lef'.

Hyeah! Le' go me dah! You hyeah me?
　　How you s'pose I gwine to steah,
When you holdin' on me dataway,
　　Wif yo' haid agin mah yeah?

Hey! You man! Who on behime dah?
　　Who dat fool a-swingin' tail?
Ef you don' un'stan' yo' business,
　　Bettah swap wiv Zulu Bale.

Dat you, Zulu? All right! Ready!
　　Shove off, niggah! Let hu' go!
Shet yo' mouf dah evahbody,
　　Ef you don' wan't full ob snow!

SUMMER.

Black man in de flat-boat,
　　Comin' down de rivah,
Fetchin' in a fat shoat,
　　An' some feeshin' livah.
Squat yo'se'f to peelin' dah, you lazy Mistah Coon!
Don' you know de promis' lan' 'll be hyeah soon?

80

Ashes of Roses

Kittle on de cross-pole,
   Singin' 'way hu' troubles;
Niggahs sneakin' into camp,
   A-totin' vegetubles.
Lawd-a-massy on mah soul, ef we gits cotched
   a-stealin'!
I weesh dat ol' fool shoat out dah 'd heish his on'ry
   squealin'.

Ovens full a-pone braid,
   In de coals a-cookin';
Chillun watahin' at de mouf,
   Stan'in' roun' a-lookin'.
Clah yo'se'f away f'um hyeah, you lazy good-fu'-
   nuffin'!
How you s'pose I gwine to cook, you stan'in' roun'
   a-snuffin'?

G'way an' lemme 'lone now—
   Hyeah! you Lucius Lee,
Drap dem yallah roas'in'-yeahs
   An' leave dem crawdads be!
Ef you don' quit yo' foolin' now, an' try to 'have
   yo'sef,
Dah 'll be one niggah in dis camp des mos' nigh beat
   to def!

Sun a-peepin' thue de trees,
   Laffin' fit to kill,—
Wondah what de rascal sees
   A-fatt'nin' in de swill?

Hi! Mistah Turkle-Soup, bettah bat yo' eye,
Som'pn mighty funny gwine happm by-m-by.

    Dah come de flat-boat,
      Shootin' in to lan'.
    Hi! Mistah Fat Shoat,
      Lemme taik yo' han'.
Mighty fine day, suh, 'cep' a trifle close,
Nevah seed a bettah fu' a fine fat roas'.

    Stiddy wiv yo' pole now,—
      Lucius, grab de livah!
    Golly, man, not dataway,
      You'll drap it in de rivah.
Ain' you got no natch'al sense? Stiddy wiv de boat—
Clah de way to glory fu' a big fat shoat!

OLD MEMORIES.

Well, sir, it jest does beat all
How things changes.   Take base ball
Now, fer instance, an' jest lay
Ourn alongside this to-day.
'Tain't the game we ust to play
Not no more'n nuthin' 'tall.
An' I'm standin' hyere to say
I p'fer the proper way.
Recollec' how you an' me
An' Buss Blazer an' the rest
Ust to play ol' A—B—C?

Gosh! take off your coat an' vest!—
Choose up sides, er one o' cat,.
Tap flies,—hyere, gimme the bat!
Scatter out there, fur's you kin—
Watch your business—three flies in!
Where's the ball at?   Hyere you go!
Don't be all day 'bout it though.
There you air!   Oh that's a daisy!
    Quick now,—muffed it.   Well I swan!
—S'pose you 'low I must be crazy,
    Way I fuss and carry on.
Why I've saw you on tip-toe,
    Yellin' 'thall yore lungs an' force,
Like a young cock tryin' to crow,
    Till you've crowed yourse'f clean hoarse.
'Member how we played an' fit?
Law, I never kin fergit.
Them wuz days the like siree
This generation 'll never see.
Alluz swimmin' in my eyes—
Same ol' trees, an' same ol' skies, —
Same ol' ever'thing, it seems,
'Ceptn' me 'at sets an' dreams.

One day las' month I wuz over
In my brother Dock's ol' clover-
Field, where his boy Will 'at's ben
Off to college had some men
With him from the city, playin'
This new ball; an' zi wuz sayin',
'Tain't no more the ol' time ball

Not no more'n nuthin' 'tall.
Who'd a-ever thought that game
Wouldn't a-always ben the same
This world over, same as then,
Base ball ferever an' amen?
Dock he's 'most ashamed o' Will
Alluz rigged out fit to kill.
College pipe, an' college hat,
College this, an' college that,—
College tell you jest can't rest.
Law-me, wisht you'd see the vest
That boy wears aroun',—my stars!
Pokey-dots, an' stripes, an' bars,—
'Nough to skeer the very face
Off a-ever'thing on the place.
Wears knee pants! an' foreign socks!—
  'Pon my word! I tol' my wife
You wouldn't b'lieve that boy wuz Dock's,
  Ef you hadn't a-knowed him all his life.

Well, zi say, Dock happened by,
Feelin' kind-a-young an' spry,
Like a ol' man does some days—
'Cordin' jest to how things lays,
On yore stumick, ef you've et
Hearty fer a couple a-meals—
You know how a feller feels—
'Tall 'pends how yore vittuls sets.
Well, Dock says, says 'e to me:
"Silas, do you know," says 'e,
"What's ben runnin' thue my head

Ever sence I tuk to bed
Las' Fall, with the rheumatiz?''
''Well, I donno, Dock,'' I says.
An' he says, says 'e, ''Ol' Hoss,''—
    Dock he calls me that fer short,—
''Me an' you has got more moss
    On our backs than what we ort.
We think,'' says 'e, ''our days is gone,
An' that brings these hyere ailments on.
An' then,'' says 'e, ''we grunt an' scold
About how we 're a-gittin' old.
It ain't no wonder we git gray
As long as we ac' thataway.
An' now,'' says 'e, without no rest,
Jest talkin' on like all possessed,
''My women-folks has went away
To ol' man Sintz's fer the day,
An' I 'm a-goin' to have a swim.''
    ''Why, Dock!'' says I, ''where at?'' says I.
''Why, down below the ol' Dead Limb,''
    Says 'e.—You recollec', don't you, Hi?
Well, Hi, we went; 'cause Dock had came
Bent on it.   No, we didn't go in.
The years ain't many, but they 've ben,
An' things is changed.   They ain't the same.
An' Dock an' me 's ben feelin' bad
Ever sence.   Things seemed so sad
'Long the ol' river bottoms now.
Things ain't the same no more, somehow.

Yes, Hi, I did fergit to tell
'Bout Will's base ball fixin's.   Well,

Dock 'splained how they make a ricket
Out a-three long sticks, an' stick it
Up at each a-them same places
Where us youngsters had the bases.
Then one boy he comes an' stan's
By a ricket, bat in han's,—
An' sech bats they got—my, oh!
But them things is modern though.
Look like paddles to canoes,
Like you've saw young Warder use
In Mad River an' Buck Crick,—
Yes, an' young Tom Kirkpatrick,
He's got some, er ust to had,
'Fore canoein' got so bad.
Well, one youngster takes a bat,
An' keeps a-retchin out like that,
So as he kin barely tech
     This hyere ricket.   Then some min,
Gittin' ready-like, to ketch,
     Scatters out as fur's they kin.
An' I tell you it's a sight—
All them figgers dressed in white,
Standin' out agin' the green,
In the ol' hay field,—I swear!—
Jest like they wuz painted there.
Only see it wunst, an' seems
Like I dremp it in my dreams.
There wuz Dock an' me alone,
Layin' there a-lookin' on,
In the shadder of the trees,
With a kind-a-lazy breeze

Jest a-stirrin', 'zif to keep
From a-droppin' off to sleep.
An' the sky seemed more 'n blue,
Jest like God wuz lookin' through,
Smilin', like He ust to do.
Whilst away off 'crost the hill
Ever'thing seemed ca'm an' still,
Like it happened long ago.
An' the hazy atmosphere,
Where the clouds wuz movin' slow,
Kind-a-blent what we could see,
Tell they wuzn't nothin' near,
'Ceptin' pore ol' Dock an' me,
Settin' in the shade alone,
Two ol' men a-lookin' on.

BILL SOMERS.

(The scene is laid in the railway station of an
Ohio town.)

Raised hyere? Was you? Don't say so?
How fur back 's that? Fourties?—Oh!
That 's ben up'ards a-right smart
'Fore my time. But mebbe you
Knowed somebody I knowed too.
There 's Bill Somers,—'member Bill?
Sad-eyed feller, long an' slim,
Kind-a-bashful? Yes, that 's him.
Come now clos't on thirty year

Sence they drug him off f'um hyere.
Come back? Yes, I b'lieve he will,
Some day. Nineteen year ol' then:
Fifty now, an' hyere I ben
A-lookin' sence I don't know when.
'Fraid not. Wisht he would though. My!
Seems sometimes like I'll jest die
A-wishin' fer him. 'Bout so high
Time his step-dad brung him hyere.
That's ben forty-some-odd year.

Folks? Bill's people? They lived East;
Daddy rich,—er wuz, at least,
'Fore he got tuk with consumption.
'Pears like must a-lost his gumption
Then, an' splutterin' round to git
Down South, fer the benefit
Of his health, he left his lands,
Et cetery, in a lorier's hands.
That's 'fore Bill wuz born, now mind,
Folks jest married, an' as blind
To this world's ornrarity
As young folks is ap' to be.
Young wife, an' this lorier
Set to hankerin' after her
From the minute he sot eyes
On her. "S'pose her husban' dies?"
Lan' sakes! Why the bare idee
Sets him plannin', and thinks'e:
"That there young greenhorn can't pull
Thue this year—onpossibul!"

Shore 'nough, 'fore Bill come, he died.
No will,—nothin; an' beside,
There's his pore young wife down South,
A-livin' jest from hand to mouth.
'Cause this lorier'd writ an' said
Times wuz hard, an' business dead,
So's he's forced to sacerfice
Ever'thing, jes' slice by slice,
Gittin' only 'nough to send
Her, but said he'd make a lend
On the rest, ef she'd take one.
La, whut else could she a-done?
Bill hed came, an' by an' by
Funds kep' gittin' mighty shy
'Bout then, an' despair set in.
Laws-a-mercy! seems a sin
Talkin' 'bout it.   Well, zi say,
Couldn't a-ben no other way—
Boy to keer fer, her a pore
Sickly widder,—ain't much more
Lef' to tell, 'cept that ol' limb
Talked her into marryin' him.

Donno much p'tic'lars 'bout
How they done 'fore he come out
West hyere, but f'um what I've learnt
Sence, 'pears like Bill's mother weren't
Keered fer like she'd ort to a-ben,
Lived nigh onto two year, then
.Seems like she wuz tuk down sick,
Got consumpted, an' died quick.

Somep'm crooked,—don't know whut—
Anyhow this stingy-gut
Of a step-dad come out West
Rather suddent.   All the rest
You know well as me, I s'pose,—
An' lots better, fur 's that goes,
Bein' older.   Him?   No; my!
Bill wuz only 'bout so high
When they brung him out.   Who?   Me?
No, I couldn't a-ben more 'n three.
All 'at I kin bring up now
'Bout them airly days is how
Bill's ol' step-dad ust to tetch
That pore boy up when he 'd ketch
Him with me; fer which said same
Neither on us wuz to blame,
Seein' how all boys likes their game.

Bill's dad never did like me.
Ner me him, fur 's that 's concerned.
We wuz pore, but I 'll be durned
Ef I wouldn't ruther be.
Well, that 's how things wuz, you see:
I liked Bill.   Bill he liked me
Better 'n I liked him, I s'pose,
Him bein' po'try an' me prose
In our get-ups,—him as fine
As a real silk fishin' line
Like you 've saw, an' me more blame
Differnter 'an he wuz same.
Guess you 'll leave me off at that,—

Ashes 'f Roses

You ketch whut I'm drivin' at.
'Course I ain't tryin' to infer
'At a feller's capabler
Of plain love jest 'cause he ain't
Bed-rid with the ol' complaint.

Bill wuz nigh come past nineteen
Time ol' man 'cused him a-stealin'
That-air money,—big an' green,
But jes' full a-kindly feelin',
Even fer that gread big mean,
Good-fer-nothin' hypocrite.
Mind you now, Bill's dad kep' eyein'
Fur ahead, like them there lyin,
Greasy-hearted rascals does.
Lorier, mind, er ust to wuz,
Only folks they didn't know
Nothin' 'tall about that though.
Well, zi say, he knowed more law
'An us folks had ever saw.
Big ol' puffed-up 'ristocrat!
Heart more blacker 'n his silk hat.
An' more slicker, too, at that.
One a-them there sancted, sly
Hypocrites.   He knowed his biz
A-plenty, as the sayin' is.
Knowed adzac'ly where to buy
Justice at, an' had the wealth
Fer to git it, an' the stealth,
An' a orly tongue, an' sech.
You know whut them there 'll fetch.

That there trial though wuz the wusst:
You jest ort a-ben to it.
That's where you'd a-up an' cussed
That ol' man.   I 'most fergit
How it wuz; but anyhow,
He set 'bout where you do now,
An' me hyere,—not quite so clost,
Mebbe,—say 'bout where that post
Is.   Well, anyhow the jury
Had went out, room hot as fury,
Folks a-waitin' so all-fired
Long 'at they wuz gittin' tired.
Then when they'd all swore they couldn't
Wait no longer, an' jest wouldn't,
Court wuz called, an' jurymin,
Long-faced, come a sulkin' in,
Tuk their places, people gone,
Court ha'f-empty, an' so on,—
Y' understand—the same ol' rule.
Well, that there ol' man a-his'n
Set there jest as ca'm an' cool,
Till he heered them words, "States prison."
Then he grinned, the blamed ol' fool!
Law-zee! I jest eetched to pick 'im
Up jest bodily, an' kick 'im
Down them court-house stairs, an' lick 'im
Down there in the street,—an' yit,
'Twouldn't a-he'ped pore Bill a bit.
There he set, them two big eyes
A-his'n lookin' 'bout the size
A-two wells, an' twict as deep.

Well, sir, I could hardly keep
From jest bawlin' right out loud
There in court.   Wisht now I had ;
Mebbe wouldn't a-felt so bad
Ever sence : seems like a cloud,
Soppin' wet with them same tears,
Ben in my head all these years.

No, I jes' set there in court,
Wonderin' ef I hadn't ort
Muster up some kind a-face,
Git up there to Bill's girl's place,
Open up, spit out the worst, —
Might a-knowed her heart 'd burst,
Seein' how she 'd bore up thue it
All, an' ef I 'd only a-knew it
Then, like I do now, you bet
I 'd a-staid right where I set.

But somehow I felt as if
My plain duty wuz to lif'
That there pore, fersaken child
Up, an' git her reconciled
To the ongitroundabul,
Do my part, be dutiful,
Then turn in an' comfort her
Like Bill's friend had ort to do.
Donno whut I thought so fer,
'Cause ef I 'd a-only knew
How much good I might a-did
By jes' stayin' 'way instid.

But I went; an' there stood Merty,
Standin' waitin' in the door.
Goodness-me! but she looked perty.
Seemed too bad 'at she wuz pore.
'Cause that there's the very stir
Bill's ol' man wuz fussin' 'bout.—
Swore he'd jest kick Bill clean out,
Ef he ever married her.
But that day,—well, I'll be blowed
Ef you ever would a-knowed
But whut she wuz jest as rich
As they make 'um. Ever' stitch
Splinter new, an' that there dress!
Call 'um travelin' gowns, I guess.
Made it all herse'f, by hand.
Ever' stitch, y' understand.
Weddin' dress to run away
An' git married in nex' day.
'Cause she knowed 'at her Bill he'd
Git cleared; said they ain't no need
Gittin' tore up 'bout it, 'cause
Loriers ner lorier's laws
Couldn't make Bill out no thief,
Never,—not to her belief.

That there'll give you some idee
How much grit I must a-had
Left, an' jest about how bad
I must a-felt there when I see
Her in that dress watchin' me.
I kin see her now this minute:

Ashes 'f Roses

My, but she looked perty in it.
Nices' shape, an' nices' size,
Like a angel,—an' them eyes!
Pore child, it wuz awful hard,
Somehow. I undone the gate,
Opened it, come in the yard,
Feelin' jest like I wuz Fate
Comin' in to drive out Hope.
Mem'ry seems to kind-a-grope
'Long in there, but seems 'at she
Looked one stiddy look at me,
Kind-a-like-a-sort-a-dream.
World went round, an' felt, an' sounded
Jest like I wuz bein' drounded
In them eyes.—An' then that scream!
My! it jest went thue an' thue
My whole soul; an' brought me to
Mighty quick, now I tell you.

Her ma must a-heered, because
When I laid her on the bed
She come runnin' in where I wuz,
Lookin' whiter 'an the dead.
Skeered me too most nigh to death,—
Couldn't seem to ketch my breath
All that night; an' that white face
A-follerin' me round ever'place.
Then there's pore ol' Bill, ferlorn,
Bein' drug off fer a crime
'At he never done no more 'n
Nothin', as they learnt in time.

Goin' on the airly train,
Too, an' there's pore Mertie layin'
Nex' to dead, an' worthless me,
No better'n whut I ort to be,
An' a hunderd meaner sech
'At the law don't never tetch.

Well, I hung around all night,
Thinkin' somep'm awful might
Happm, tell on towords daylight,
I snuck down hyere to this ol' station,
Sad-like, to tell Bill good-bye,
Fer three year to come; an' my !
Seemed as long as all creation
Waitin' hyere without no one,
'Ceptin' jest myse'f to run
On an' talk to, like I done
Fer a hour er two, er three,
Er mebbe four, it seemed to me.

By an' by I heered some talk
Outside, an' got up to walk
Out an' see, an' run agin
Bill, han'cuffed between two min.
One wuz Sheriff Lane, an' t'other
Might a-ben his big twin brother,
Jedgin' by his size an' stren'th.
Leedle longer though, in len'th,
Mebbe, an' a trifle wider,
An' more self-come-satisfider,
Jedgin' by the easy way

He turned off an' walked away
When he seen me.—But 'zi say,
I wuz interested in
Seein' Bill, an' not strange min.
But jest then I seen a light,
An' a ingine hove in sight,
Round the curve, by Thompson's mill,
Steamed a-past us fit to kill,
Slowed up to a dead stand-still,
Then stood pantin' whilse she drank
Water outo' the waterin'-tank.

Pore ol' Bill.—I seen him go
That there mornin', an' I know
I'd lots ruther went to prison
Place a-him. 'T'uz awful still:
I leant over, an' says, "Bill,"—
Bill he tuk my hand in his'n.
"Bill," I says,—an' then it seemed
Jest like ever'thing wuz steamed,
An' kind-a-blurred, an' turnin' round.
Then I heered a rushin' sound,
Like steam 'scapin', an' the train
Pullin' out, an' Bill says, "Jim,"
An' looked up, an' me at him.
They wuz worlds a-unspoke pain
In them eyes.

        Well, next I knowed
I wuz standin' on the track
Lookin'; an' a whissle blowed

Way, way off, an' brought me back
To myse'f; an' think-says-I:
"That there sounds jest like a groan
From the dead;" and donno why,
I ain't skeered to be alone
'Fore daylight that way, but my!
That there sound does han't me so
When I hear a whissle moan
Way off that way,—I donno,
But somehow jes' seems to go
To the marrer of my bone;
'Specially ef I'm alone
Somewheres, like—there! hear that now,
Off there? Must be some ol' cow
On the track, as Bill'd say.
But it don't 'fec' me that way
Sence that night.

The train Bill rid
On that mornin', sir, wuz slid
Off the track, an' robbed, an' burnt
By train robbers, as wuz learnt
That there very day. Some b'lieves
Bill wuz rescued by the thieves,
An' tuk off an' helt fer ransom,
Thinkin' they'd git somep'm han'some
From the ol' man, but it 'pears
Like he's meaner fer his years
Than they s'posed, an' some folks fears
Bill wuz massacreed, er shot,
Er sech like, but I reckon not.

Som'pm tells me 'twon't be long
'Fore we meet, an' right er wrong,
Don't mind much whut people say,
I'm on hands hyere ever' day
Train time, waitin' fer ol' Bill.
Years now, but I'm hopin' still.

Then I've got his dad's estate
An' all, to hold an' 'ministrate
Jest fer him. They ain't no heirs
'Cept him livin' anywheres.
An' I've wrote this country thue
Fer him, like I'd orto do,
Waited an' philoserphized,
Inquired, hunted, advertised
In the papers,—Lord knows whut
I ain't done, an' like as not
Some day I'll spend all I got.

Mertie? Yes, she's livin', yes.
Yes, indeed; an I don't guess
She's fergot; 'cause that there dress
Lays upstairs, all putt away
Smooth. I'm sayin' jest to-day:
S'pose Bill does come back fer her
Some these days—what would she do?
"Why, I'd stand right hyere by you,
Like I'm standin' now," says she,
"Happy, like I'd ort to be."
Yes, she's kep' house now fer me
An' my boys sence mother died.

Up an' at pore mother's side
To the last, jest like she's ben
Fer thirty year,—a faithful frien'
To rich an' pore,—they 're all the same
To her,—she never lays no blame
To no one,—sympathacious soul.
"Heaven," she 'lows, "is all min's goal."

Pore ol' Bill! I wonder where
He's at. Mebbe in his grave.
Hope I 'll meet him over there,
Where the past is all fergave.
Gread big-hearted, awk'ard cow.
Give the world to see him now.
No one ain't a bit like him,
Quiet-like, an' tall, an' slim.
I loved ol' Bill, I did. An' he,—
I b'lieve he hankered after me.
Best hearted boy they ever were.
The only man they ever were
Fer sech a character as her.

THE DIFFUSION OF LEARNING.

Wunst me 'n Willie Smif an' Joe
Ollic was iss playin' show
In ar back yard wunst, an' nen
Iss me 'n Willie played p'ten'
Like we 're bray-big acterbats,
Whut they don't wear shoes, ner hats,

Ner nuffin' on 'm, 'cep' iss skin
On neir laigs.   Ma says 't'sa sin
Cause my pa he taked me there
One day, but my pa don't care.
You ist orto hear him swear!
My ma she iss leaves pa be
When he's cross, an' my pa he
Says my ma she'd better had;
Nen her iss feels awful bad,
'Cause her groans an' says "Oh dear!"
Nen her iss cries, pitinear.
                Does yourn?

It was only ist a pin
An' a opple to git in
Ar show nen, an' Joe he bringed
His canerry-bird 'at singed
Mostest tunes!   Nen nat ol' Bud
Unkenzander slinged some mud
Over ar back olly fence
Nen, an' iss maked me commence
Fightin', 'cause my pa says he
Wants me to, an' my ma she
Called me in an' paddled me.
Nen ne boys is all iss mad
An' goed home, an' I bin bad
Till my ma iss set an' cried
Wight out loud.   Nen I iss tried
Awful hard to be good, nen
Purty soon a'm good again.
                Are you?

Are you got a funny pa
Like a'm got? Say, is your ma
A-livin'? Charlie Ollic's ain't,
'Cause she's turned into a saint.
Is too! Guess I orto know!
Charlie went an' telled me so
Wunst hisself, up on my bed
One day, when we're playin' dead.
Yes, 'n' he says if childern plays
Like ney're dead, nen some nese days
They're gits growed nat way an' stays.
Yes sir, 'cause my baby brover
Gitted growed nat way, 'n' my muvver
Tried to made him git unwaked,
An' couldn't, nen is cried, an' maked
Me cry too; nen Gramma, her
Comed an' taked me home wif her—
        Her did.

Yes, 'n' I swored a bad word when
They was comp'ny eatin' nen
At her house, an' gramma she
Iss looked th'ough her specs at me,
Nen iss pushed back my high-cher,
An' telled me come on wif her
To ne worsh-house, where her cat's
Got some baby kittens at,
Way up on a high place, where
Nasty me'cine is up nere.
Nen her put some burny lye
In my mouf, an' by and by

102

I iss couldn't iss but cry.
'Cause it hurted, too, wight in
Where 's my tongue an' teef an' skin.
Nen her says: "Nem bad words 'bout
Purty nigh clean all burned out
By vis time ;" nen her iss preached
Longer 'n' ar preacher, 'n' teached
Me most fings 'at he don't know
Like gramma.   Her knows 'um, though.
Yes, 'n' my mamma says they 're so.
       Her knows.

Yes, 'n' they 's a Good Man lives
Way up in the sky 'at gives
Peoples vittuls an' coal an' wood
An' ever'fing if they 're be 's good.
An' he iss lissuns fer boys 'at swears,
An' hides, an' iss looks ever'wheres.
Yes, 'n' you better say your prayers
An' mind grown folks, er you 'll git saw,
Nen you can't go wif my gramma
When her goes.   A 'm go' to see
Iss how gooder as I kin be;
An' iss a-go' to romp, an' run,
An' be wight good, iss like I done
At gramma's, an' iss play fun.
I nain't never go' to swore
Nasty bad words nany more
Tell I git a bray big man
Like my pa is—nen I can,
       Can't I?

THERE, THERE, 'T WILL NOT BE LONG.

There, there, 't will not be long;
   Weep no hot tears for me, love,
For I will sing a happy song
   Whene'er I think of thee, love.
   Whene'er I think of thee,
   And often that shall be.
There, there, dear heart, 't will not be long;
   Weep no more tears for me.

Say me a sweet farewell.
   Oh love, look up and kiss me.
And tell me now, as thou canst tell,
   Thus wilt thou always miss me?
   Oh wilt thou weep and say,
   "My love is far away?"
There, there, be patient, I will come;
   I go, but not to stay.

Now I am with thee, dear;
   To-night, when thou art lonely,
Then thou wilt say, "If he were here,"
   And "Oh, if I had only."
   Come, we must not be weak;
   Smile through thy tears and speak.
There, I will wipe away thy grief
   And soothe thy poor, scarred cheek.

There, there, 't will not be long;
   Be happy now for me, love.

I go because I must.   Be strong.
  I will come back to thee, love.
  I will come back to thee,
  I will come back to thee,
Good-bye, sweetheart, 'twill not be long.
  Be brave, and watch for me.

WRITTEN FOR A FRIEND.

Blind? Going blind? O God, what have I done
  That I no more may see the glorious birth
Of happy days? No more for me the sun
  Shall gild with splendor all the glittering earth.
What have I done that Thou shouldst strike me blind?
  Oh, speak to me, for I have better ears
To hear Thy voice. Aye, and a clearer mind
  To see through Thy great goodness. Calm my fears.
How strange that in this darkness I should feel
  Thy presence nearer now than e'er before.
The things of earth that did so long conceal
  Thy face from me, conceal Thee now no more.
Blind? Aye, and happy too; for now I see
No more myself, oh God, but only Thee.

TO A MOTHER.

Thou art the chosen mother of a son,
  Sent to thy care from Heaven, as thou wert sent,
To carry on the work that Christ begun,
  Who came from Heaven to show us what God meant.

As Mary was exalted by the event
　Which gave us Jesus, so if thou give us one
To do God's will, thou too shalt rise content
　Above thy days; thy cup shall overrun
With very joyance; and the grateful tears
　Of happy motherhood shall lift thy soul
Like some fair cloud above the sea of years.
　Thou, by thy loving precepts, shalt control
Men, and their deeds, and thyself glorify.
Our noble mothers have not lived to die.

KISS ME GOOD-NIGHT.

Kiss me good-night.　Here where alone I sit,
　Before the fire, and all is strange and still,
Methinks I see thee where the shadows flit,
　Looking at me, until mine own eyes fill
And stream with bitter longing.　Why so white?
Your hand—speak to me dear—kiss me good night.

When I am gone, oh do you think of me,
　As I of thee, and reach with yearning hands
And aching heart through the long months to be,
　Wondering if he who loves thee understands?
Oft at the window in the cold moonlight
I look with faithful eyes out through the winter night.

Kiss me good-night.　For He Who gave my dove
　May take her ere the morrow for His own.

And oh, who then is left for me to love,
  When thou art gone, and I am left alone.
I must not dream of death : it is not right.
I will be happy, dear—kiss me good-night. Good-night.

WHEN WINTER COMES.

When Win'er comes, an' Summer goes,
    And Win'er comes,
My mamma she 'most alluz knows
    When Win'er comes.
'Cause nen her darns my un'erclo'es,
An' buys me boots wif copper toes ;
An' says, "Now come in 'fore you 're froze."
    When Win'er comes.

My mamma says boys alluz grows,
    When Win'er comes.
Yes, an' her says ne badness shows
    When Win'er comes.
'Cause little boys comes in 'mos' froze,
An' warms neirselves, an' never close
Ne doors behind 'um when ney 're goes,
    When Win'er comes.

I never go fwif bruvver 'Brose
    When Win'er comes,
Away out huntin' where he goes,
    When Win'er comes,
'Cause nen ne snow, why it iss snows,
An' ne win', why it iss blows an' blows ;
An' makes ne tears wun down my nose,
    When Win'er comes.

WHY SHOULD I SHED ONE TEAR?

Why should I shed one tear
  For these poor, dumb, white flowers?
Or even for the dull, dead year
Around me here?
  The joy to hope is ours.
To hope the time is near
When we, my precious dear,
  Shall drag no more the sad, unwilling hours
Through weary day, and week, and month, and year.

Oh, let us hope, not grieve;
  Though the nest in the thorn be deserted,
And the cold winds sob and heave,
Like friends that cleave
  In vain to their departed,
Still let us hope, not grieve.
The joy is ours to believe.
  In spring the little birds that be true-hearted
Will come and find their mates, and sing, and weave.

WITH YOU, SWEET LOVE.

I'm spending the evening with you, my love,
  After a long, hard day,—
Just as I always do, sweet love,
  Though many a mile away;
And I stay as I used to stay,
  Till the hours are gray and still,
And I think and think of the happy day
  When this shall all be real.

108

Ashes of Roses

When this shall all come true, my dear,
  And we shall be happy then.
When the long, long wait is through, O dear,
  And I come back home again;
And you meet me and kiss me then,
  And the guests are all gone at last,
And we sit by the fire alone and plan,
  As we used to, love, in the past.

And we'll dream till the night is gone, O love,
  But the rest shall still remain;
Till the silence hints of dawn, sweet love, ·
  But it shall hint in vain;
For we'll feel no more the pain
  Of parting at dead of night,
And roses, and not tears, shall stain
  The pillows pale and white.

ROSES.

Two flowers remain, one red, one white,
  Of those you sent me Christmas day.
The rest, like friends of one brief night,
  Have faded from their sides away
And now, like lovers old and gray,
  That sit in silence, hand in hand,
Waiting the flare of life's last ray
  To light them to a better land,

Here in the twilight still they stand,
　　And I, alone, to watch them die;
And wonder if 'tis God's command
　　That these two flowers are you and I.
The room grows dark; outside, the winter rain
Beats, like a troubled heart, against the pane.

POPULAR PROVIDENCE.

Dey wuz once a ol' coon in de top ob er tree;
　　An' I thinks to mahse'f, says I:
De Lawd pu'tended dat coon fu' me.''
　　Lemme tol' you de reason why.

Dah's Mistah Coon, an' hyeah stan's me,
　　Wif a gun in mah han's des' so;
An' I ups an' I aims at de top ob dat tree,
　　Wha' Mistah Coon is, you know.

Now when dey's a coon at de en' ob yo' gun,
　　An' you bunches yo' eye an' squint,
An' pulls de triggah, why ten to one
　　Mistah Coon 'll taik de hint.

Kaze de Lawd's allers got His han' in de game,
　　'Nelse we'd nach'ly stahve fu' def.
An' when dat's de case, an' you misses yo' aim,
　　Why,—you oughtah be 'shamed yo'se'f.

110

AT DIM TWILIGHT.

At dim twilight,
When woodlands darken,
I love to hearken
To the night.
While far away
Across the meadows,
The swallows play
Like flitting shadows,
And children's voices,
Like the day,
Far in the distance
Die away,—
Away, away, away, away,
Far in the distance
Dying away.

The hour of prayer
Thus steals around me,
And God has found me
Waiting there.
And oh how sweet
A joy to own,
That I may meet
My God alone,
When all the noises
Of busy day
Doze into silence,
And die away.
Away, away, away, away,
Peace to the world,
Farewell to the day.

PARTED.

I must be gone, my dear, the hour is late,
  And I must rest me for the coming day.
Would we were wed to-night.— How can I wait?
  What shall I do to drag the months away?
Good-night.   There, now, good-night,— I cannot stay.
  I must be gone.   And yet, oh cruel Fate,
Why is it those who love the most are they
  Who for the longest times must separate?
Yet it must be: God's will and ours are one,
Since we have freely said His will, not ours, be done.

He gave our love; we are in training now
  To enjoy the life we long for.   After while,
When He has shown us, we shall wonder how
  We failed to see it all; and we shall smile
To find ourselves alone and face to face,
  Happy at last, and with the eternal right
From God himself to keep our hushed embrace
  With throbbing raptures through the silent night.
Then there shall come no rude disturbance nigh
To tear our souls apart.   Till then, O Love, good-bye.

JOE SNOW.

Who dat you lookin' fo'?   Mistah Snow?
  No sich man in mah haid.
Nevah were, no suh, fu' as I know,
'Ceptin' one 'at disanpeahed long time ago,
An' he nevah did come back no mo',
  An' mammy 'low he 's daid.

Joseph Snow? Well dat beats sin.
  Dah 's somepin de mattah wif mah recollection.
You know whah he come f'om, an' who 's his kin,
  An' all about his fambly connection?
Heah, take a cheer. Mammy she ain't in;
  She wasn't a-havin' no expection
A-strangers a-comin' dis time a-day,
She 's des gone off down dataway.
Ef de eetch ob mah bah feet don't lie
She 'll be comin' back now by-m-by.

You got dat name right now, fo' sho'?
  'Kaze dey ain't no sich aroun'.
Dey is some Snow folks lives berlow,
  Des on de aidge a-town,
De ones I tellin' you while ago
  Which de ol' man ain't been foun'.

I was only 'long 'bout two yeah ol',
  An' I ain't nevah hyeahed
Des whut 's de trouble, 'cep' I heern tol'
  Dat he natch'ly disanpeahed.
Den Joe, he was bo'n, an' bress yo' soul
  He look lak he wuz skeered.

Ol' Joe Snow is dat dre'ful slow
  He kain't mek up his min'
Whethah he 's in de humern race,
  O' des taggin' on behin'.
Nevah did see sich a crazy man;
  He ain't got a spec a-sense;

Evah time you' goin' down pas' his house
  He a-settin' dah on de fence.
Des a settin' dah disaway,
  A-lookin' des lak a ha'nt.
Lawzee! but dat man look po';
  He gittin' dat thin an' ga'nt
Dey ain't nuffin' lef' a-his 'riginal se'f
  'Ceptin' des a bag a-bones.
Nevah say nuffin' to no man,
  Des set on de fence an' groans.

Dey ain't no persons livin' dah
  'Ceptin' him an' his ol' maw;
An' it taik all de scratchin' she kin do
  Fo' to fill dat niggah's craw.
Folks 'lows she's a smaht ol' lady, too,
  An' so were ol' Joe's paw.

         *   *   *

Oh mistah! I fo'gotten to tell you!
Ef a braid-big dawg come up an' smell you,
Doan' be a-skeered,—dat dawg's all right.
You leave him 'lone, an' he'll treat you white.

FALL ROSES.

These flowers should not make me sad :
  Red flowers are for love, you say.
Yet if flowers were all I had,
  Here so far away,
Though they be sent by thee,
  Kissed and sent for my delight,

Though I know thou lovest me,
  Be they red or white,
Still if flowers were all I had,
Tell me, how could I be glad?

Autumn flowers and autumn leaves
  Linger but a little while;
Then when Indian Summer grieves,—
  Nay, but let us smile.
He Who made these flowers to die
  Made our love to live forever;
Though the day pass away,
  True love dieth never.
Let us then be glad, and smile;
Love is growing all the while.

LEAN MAN'S PREJUDICE.

I hates to see a man maik a hog of hisse'f,—
  Er a woman, too, fu' dat mattah.
Some folks des eats twell dey ain't nuffin' lef';
  Den licks ha'f way thue de plattah.
But it's gen'ly de swine dat's mos' fattened to def
  Dat tries so ha'd to git fattah.

Some folks kin'-a-'lows ef dey's clean hog fat,
  F'um a-eatin', an' a-sleepin', an' a-drinkin',
Dat dey's got mo' brains in de top ob dey hat
  Fu' to set fool folks a-blinkin'.
But I'd lak to know wha' de worl''d be at
  Ef de fat folks done all de thinkin'.

A LITTLE BOY.

Mamma, where you goin'—say,
    Mamma?
    Aw mamma,
Stay at home wif me? Please stay,
    Mamma.
I 'll be quiet. I won't play
Noisy games no more all day.
Honest trufe! Please don't go 'way,
    Will you,
    Mamma?

What makes you go calling for,
    Mamma?
    Say mamma,
You don't like me nany more,
    Mamma.
'Cause if you did you wouldn't go
Where they 's clubs, an' to the show
Ever' night. You 'd stay home though,
    Wouldn't you,
    Mamma?

Take me wif you, won't you, please
    Mamma?
    Please, mamma,
Take me wif you? I won't tease,
    Mamma.
I 'd lots ravver stay at home

If you stay.   But when you're gone
I ist always feel alone.
>   Don't I,
>   Mamma?

I don't like to stay wif nurse,
>   Mamma.
>   'Cause mamma,
When I'm cross she makes me worse.
>   Mamma.
I try hard to not to cry,
'Cause I love you.   By an' by
You'll love me, too, when I die,
>   Won't you,
>   Mamma?

IN COUSIN ETTA'S BIRTHDAY BOOK.

The rudest prospect, softened in the mist
Of dreamy-sweet September, faintly kissed
At early sunrise, melts to amethyst.

And paths that lead into that hazy scene,
However rough the vales that intervene,
Suggest a world whose like has never been.

So mayest thou see me in my early days,
A doubtful vale, whose many winding ways
Give promise of some good beyond the haze.

EPH.

Y'oughtah seen ol' Eph yistiddy—
　Hya-ha-ha! Thought I'd die!
Dat ol' soak were mo' 'an giddy—
　Hya-ha-ha! Thought I'd die!
Hyeah comes him ercross de clearin',
Singin' lak he ain't a-keerin'
Which away his laigs is steerin'—
　Hya-ha-ha! Thought I'd die!

Thinks I, "Hyeah's yo' chance fu' fun"—
　Hya-ha-ha! Thought I'd die!
"Watch me mek dat niggah run."
　Hya-ha-ha! Thought I'd die!
Jes' slipped off mah mule an' hitch
In de woods an' cut er switch.
It were gittin' da'k as pitch.
　Hya-ha-ha! Thought I'd die!

I jes' gove mah eye er squint—
　Hya-ha-ha! Thought I'd die!
Clean chucked full a-debilmint—
　Hya-ha-ha! Thought I'd die!
Eph kep' comin' 'cross de stubbles,
Cogertatin' bout he troubles,
Seein' evahthing by doubles—
　Hya-ha-ha! Thought I'd die!

I come sneakin' up behime—
　Hya-ha-ha! Thought I'd die!

Hol' on, honey, gimme time!
  Hya-ha-ha! Thought I'd die!
I jes' gripped dat ol' tho'n stick,
Ups an' fotch dat man a lick
Right ercross his ol' bed tick —
  Hya-ha-ha! Thought I'd die!

Say! dat coon did paw de groun'!
  Hya-ha-ha! Thought I'd die!
Nevah did stop to look aroun'!
  Hya-ha-ha! Thought I'd die!
He jes' fotch a yell an' flew!
An' me aftah! I tell you
Dat drunk man did run fu' true.
  Hya-ha-ha! Thought I'd die!

I jes' hat to lay an' roll!
  Hya-ha-ha! Thought I'd die!
Clean outrunned me, bress yo' soul!
  Hya-ha-ha! Thought I'd die!
I jes' laffed dah to mahse'f
Twell I couldn' ketch mah bref. —
Say! Dat coon were skeered to def.
  Hya-ha-ha! Thought I'd die!

ODE TO GERTRUDE.

Lo, now the worries of the day are o'er;
  And sick with solitude,
I seek my lonely room, and shut the door,
  And yield me to my mood.

My love.   My love.   My nearest, dearest love
   In all this world to me,—
Not that I find this side of Heaven above
   One that compares with thee,
   However dear the ones I love may be.   `
No, no, not that.
'T is that my pent-up soul doth cry aloud
   From out this word-dark sea that floods my
      brain,
Only to send a vague, unmeaning cloud
   Of empty words to fall like passing rain
   Upon thy thirsting soul, that thou, in vain,
   May'st try and soothe my pain.

Oh that I felt thy form, thy breathing form,
   Here in my arms—thy face,
Blinded in passion with my own, and warm,
   In this cold, empty place.
My lonely being burns me with desire
   To be with thee to-night,
My pulses throb and beat with futile fire—
   I reach out in the night!
I seek thy lips!   I crush the lifeless air!
Thou art not there.
   My spirit sobs and grieves till early light.
   Ah, love, dost thou too feel this same despair?

Oh sweet despair of words!   Oh painful bliss!
   To reach the very hush
      Where silence fails,

And language, resurrected with a kiss,
  Can only halt, and blush.—
    My spirit wails
And cries aloud for thee!
O love! My love! My life that is to be!
My very death! Ah, me.

    ❦   A MOTHER.

Gracious-goodness-sakes-alive!
Land-a-mercy! Why you'll drive
Me start crazy some these days!
Go on now an' have yore ways.
But don't come to me fer no
Symp'thy when you stub yore toe!

Hear that young'un carry on!
Stubbed his toe agin—I knew it!
Didn't I say you'd go an' do it?
Child-a-goodness! Well I swan!
Come to mamma,—there, don't cry,
It'll stop bleedin' by an' by.

There now, run an' play agin.
Hyere's a napple. Now take keer.
Bless yore heart, of course you kin,—
But walk keerful. Bless the dear.
Boys is boys sence Adam—law!
Sweeter child I never saw.

121

A LITTLE SONG FOR GERTRUDE.

A little girl made her lover
A calendar of days,
With a dainty little cover
All done in browns and grays.
All done in browns and grays, you know,
All done in browns and grays.

The cover was a little flower.—
A pansy, I believe.
However, I will not be sure:
Tale bearers will deceive.
Tale bearers will deceive, you know,
Tale bearers will deceive.

The little maiden tied it,
And with a trembling hand,
Made pictures all inside it,
That he would understand.
That he would understand, you know,
That he would understand.

And then that pretty maiden
Took from her fluttering breast,
Where all such things lie hidden,
An envelope, addressed.
An envelope, addressed, you know,
An envelope, addressed.

She sweetly sealed and kissed it,
And ran oh, many blocks,

And lovingly dismissed it
  Into a letter-box.
  Into a letter-box, you know,
  Into a letter-box.

Don't ask me now who got it.
  That wasn't meant for you.
I told you all about it,—
  Or all I wanted to.
  Or all I wanted to, you know,
  Or all I wanted to.

I LOVE THEE.

I love thee, love, with all the love
  My ardent, burning being
Can feel, can tell, is capable of,
  Or even thou of seeing.
I love thee, oh I love thee,
  There can be none before.
God only is above thee,
  And Him we both adore.

I love thee, love.   Must I confess
  That I have failed to tell thee?
Oh let thine own pure loveliness
  Sweeten the words I spell thee.
I love thee, oh I love thee.
  The same words o'er and o'er,
Aye, I do more than love thee,
  God only loves thee more.

NIGHT.

With military pomp and strut,
  And sound of rolling drums,
Before his dark-eyed Spanish troops
  The Captain-General comes.

I see him with his rigid jaw,
  His cruelty, and spite.
My heart goes out to the hungry men
  In Cuba's camps to-night.

REGRET.

The river of years flows out to sea,
  Into the deep, dark night of never.
My youth is drifting away from me,
  And shall return no more forever.
Stop! stop! thou ever-flowing river,
  Bring me the days misspent and gone.
But ah, it floweth on forever,
  Forever and ever it floweth on.
And I long for the days and the years misspent,
  Till my life is becoming an old man's story.
Oh why have I not been content
  To work for God and forget the glory!
Ring out, ye sea bells, over the waves!
  Shriek and wail ye whistles of warning!
The grand old world is built on graves,
  And I shall do better to-morrow morning.

How shall I wait till to-morrow morning?
'T is scarce midnight by the struggling moon.
And the day that is gone is never returning;
And the morrow never comes too soon.
Oh soul! make friends with the busy days,
And follow no more the flying years.
Sleep and toil, for the present stays,
And the past and future are full of tears.

OFFHAND REPLIES.

I.

Do thy best, and leave the rest
To Him Who loves the unexpressed.
He gave thy mind the truth to find,
Thy conscience, lest thou still be blind.
Think first is all He asks of all.—
In stubbornness alone we fall.
Or standing still in faith until
The Lord some prophecy fulfill.
But weigh and prove before thou move,
Then fit thee in thy proper groove:
Now, lest thou make a sad mistake,
Look to thy conscience and keep awake.

II.

If I were only you,
    And you were only I,
I would do as you do,
    And you would wonder why.

125

III.

The better the master the better the man;
  The better the man the better the work.
The meaner the master the meaner the man;
  The meaner the man the meaner the shirk.
But the better the man in spite of the master,
The greater the man in the night of disaster.
  The better either because of the other,
  The better for everybody, my brother.   .

IV.

  Believe in men as they should be :
  You cannot tell what they would be.
  And what they are no man can see.

V.

Nevah could mek a speech,
  'Case mah brains won't wu'k, somehow.
When I stan's on mah feet dey ain't kin reach
  Twell de top ob mah ol' hay-mow.
An' a man kain't mek no sawt of a speech
  Wif he brains all down in he shoes.—
I reckon I'd rathah hyeah you-all preach.
  I begs to be excuse'.

VI.

  Better glad out of due season
  Than sad without good reason.

VII.

No word that holy men have writ
Can teach us how to pray,
Unless at God's own feet we sit,
And learn it just as they.

VIII.

De mos' wisdomes' thoughts is do ones dat you think
When yo' flat on yo' back an' cain't sleep a wink.

IX.

A beach, a girl, a man.
'T was so since time began.

X.

The waves wash over the strand,
    Over the hopes of men ;
If you see a pearl in the shifting sand,
    Rescue it there and then.
If the waves take it out of the reach of your hand,
    It never comes back again.

XI.

God is my religion,
    My conscience is my creed,
Jesus and all men my brothers,
    What more do I need?

"THEY CRY UNTO THE LORD IN THEIR TROUBLES."

Night comes: the shadowy farms expand
    Like maps from town to town.
The city sleeps; and over all
    The placid moon looks down.

Day breaks: the farmer calls his sons
    To turn the fertile soil;
And in the city honest men
    Go forth to honest toil.

Man eats the pleasant bread of peace;
    And when still evening creeps
Upon the world, he goeth home,
    Tired out; night comes; he sleeps.

Sweet is the peace our fathers bought
    With their own blood for us.
How can we think of all they did,
    And treat the Cubans thus?

Their struggle has been just as brave:
    Their cause is just the same;
Their tyrants even worse than those
    Our fathers overcame.

God save them at this awful time
    Their wives and little ones,
While all the world stands looking on,
    With polished swords and guns.

PRIDE DOETH, PRIDE RUETH.

She stopped to scold some naughty boys,
  Who watched a naughty cat,
That eyed a bird that never stirred
  From the limb whereon he sat.
On another limb not far from him
  Crouched a spider, big and fat,
Who had his eye on a dragon fly
  That lay in wait for a gnat.
The gnat came by, and the dragon fly
  Had soon been glad thereat,
But the spider bold on him took hold,
  And heigh! for a bloody spat.
The spider clung with tooth and tongue,
  Like an evil insect rat,
And the other thing, with claw and sting,
  Came back at the ugly brat!
They had it there, that long-legg'd pair,
  But the bird soon had them pat,
And the whole outfit made a dainty bit
  For the sly old whiskered cat.
The eager boys let loose their noise,
  And screeched in sharp and flat!
The maid lent lungs and pushed the bungs
  Into her sweet tear vat.
But her pleadings loud on that hard crowd
  Were not worth half a sprat,
For they only winked a wicked wink
  And the louder laughed; whereat,

Up spoke a youth whose face was truth:
"Cats eat birds: what of that?
They live thereby; but pray tell why
You wear one on your hat."

DUTY.

Do your part with all your heart,
　　Whatever else may be;
And I will always try to do
　　More than is meant for me.

Still if I find you fall behind,
　　With more than you can do,
I'll shoulder more; but if I fail,
　　That duty rests with you.

So may we in true duty, love,
　　Our highest hopes attain,
Which either one, if left alone,
　　Had striven for in vain.

TO MY MUSE.

There was a time when disappointments rung
Their sad, perpetual bass to all I sung.
How changed.   The image of thy presence here
Makes my poor strains come sweeter, and more
　　clear.
I sing my best, dear love, when dreaming thou art
　　near.

It used to be, too, when my eyes were dim,
I looked to God in faith, but saw not Him.
Now, dearest Gertrude, when I kneel to pray,
Though I do feel in truth each word I say,
Yet thy sweet face is there, and will not go away.

God knows. 'T is well. He hath made manifest
In thee, my hope, all that is pure and best.
I know Him now. Before thou camest to me
I knew Him not. I had not learned to see.
He bade me look: I looked, and saw Him, love, in
    'thee.

Thou art my inspiration; for I find
He makes His dwelling in thy lowly mind.
There by that sacred book where I may read
And find the consolation that I need,
I see my God enthroned in purity, my creed.

Aye, you may blush for modesty, my love,
As blushes to her mate the modest dove.
Yet will I sing thy praises while we live,
Lest He Who has no more like thee to give,
Should exercise too soon His kind prerogative.

I live in fear and hope, as one who sees
Successive clouds pass over by degrees;
Not knowing which the blessings may contain,
Which the deluge, and which the gentle rain.
Yet I have faith, sweetheart, that we shall meet again.

My mood doth vary with thy varying steps :
Now sinks my soul, now trembles, and now leaps !
When thou art with me all the world is bright.
But oh, when thou art gone, how dark the night.
How long it seems to wait the coming of the light.

Ah, infinitely kind our God must be,
Who could create such perfectness for me.
Sweet, lovely revelation of His grace,
Compared with whom all things are commonplace,
What joy can compensate the absence of thy face.

Yet there were times when disappointments rung
Their dull, disheartening bass to all I sung.
Now, wearied that a fruitless day has flown,
I smile to God, and in an undertone
Breathe thy sweet name, Gertrude, and I am not
    alone.

A PEAR-BLOSSOM IN EARLY MARCH.

Yes, I am pleased, but not surprised,
   That you have sent me, Gertrude dear,
This blossom, blown and sacrificed
   At this strange time of year.

Were I a bud, and kissed by thee
   In cold midwinter, there would flow
Through me such waves of ecstacy
   That I would blush and blow.

132

Ashes of Roses

And I, and every bud would burst,
  And watch, while you removed your glove,
In wild suspense to be the first,
  The one that you should touch and love.

And oh, if still thou deemed me best,
  And plucked me from the frozen stem,
And held me next thy glowing breast,
  How might I pity them.

How might I pity, as I do,
  The unloved buds that cannot bloom,
Because no Gertrude comes to woo
  Their petals from the living tomb.

Then take me back—take back this one.
  For I have dreamed this one is I.
Oh take me back, lest here alone,
  Unloved by thee, I die.

So lay me on thy bosom, sweet,
  And think thee then, if I were this,
How thy sweet lips and mine would meet
  In one prolonged, impassioned kiss.

And I shall follow by and by,
  And we shall know that pure delight
When there are none but you and I,
  And God, and hush, and night.

Oh hopeful day ! Ah, Gertrude dear,
  Would I could force the buds of time
To blossom into month and year,
  As feelings blossom into rhyme.

Then might our dreams — no, dearest, no.
  And yet, — not yet, my precious dove.
Be patient, and the buds will blow.
  God has His time, and we our love.

AN ANONYMOUS ATTACK.

To criticise is first to appreciate.
  (But boys' ideas, like their clothes, shrink on
    them.)
Only the great can comprehend the great.
  All have opinions, but the wise think on them.
Let witics joke my lines, — I 'll join the laugh.
  And critics scratch me if they must, — I'll spare
    them.
They cannot tell me all my faults by half ;
  Nor recognize my virtues, save they share them.
Bless all the fun there is at my expense.
  Bless all the good that everybody does.
The inoffensive cannot take offense.
  If I am ever great, God is the cause.
  If ever weak, love me for what I was.
Judge not, lest ye love not : ye are the conse-
    quence.

SPRING.

Have you heard the robins singing,
　　　Gertrude dear?
Have you heard the robins singing?
　　　Spring is here.
I can feel my own joy ringing,
In their glad, incessant singing,
In their loud, melodious singing,—
　　　Kiss me, dear.

Summer's coming,—I feel showers
　　　Through and through.
I can breathe the breath of flowers,
　　　Love, can you?
None, I know; but the sun is brighter,
And the air seems soft and lighter.
See, the very clouds sail whiter
　　　In the blue.

Soon the trees will spread their shadows,
　　　Cool and deep,
Where the hazy, drowsy meadows
　　　Doze and sleep.
Then these little birds, confiding
All their love in secret hiding,
Will have built their wee abiding
　　　Where we peep.

Come let us go and wander,
　　　You and I,

Up the old lane winding yonder
        To the sky.
There we'll stroll and dream together
Of the nest we too shall feather
In the happy summer weather
        By and by.

TO A WINDFLOWER.

Poor, frail little windflower,
    Crushed between the leaves
Of this letter from my love,
    He who preforgives
All that I am guilty of,
Take thy little soul above.

Back to Him, sweet windflower,
    Yield thy fragrant breath.
Thou who camest here to me,
    Lovely, though in death,
Thou who art as fair as she,
Ah, but no, that cannot be.

Ah, I knew a windflower,
    Pure and fair as thou.
But the good are very frail.
    She is withered now.
Sister of my wayward years,
Ah, I wonder if she hears.

136

"CUBA LIBRE!" *

Oh how sweet the secret summons to the breathless
    Halls of Fame,
Where the eager world awaits us — loud to praise, and
    quick to blame.
Hot to hail the coming hero: "Who the next? Who
    will it be?"
Ah, how nervously we mutter, "Wait — be patient — I
    am he."
"Patience — patience — I am coming! Oh I have no
    uniform —
They will call me boy, and—" Listen! 'tis the hush
    before the storm.
How we swallow — how the heart beats — yet what
    confidence we feel!
None can do our duty for us; we must act; and act
    with zeal.
Ready now, — be brave, O spirit, — friends enough will
    follow on.
We cannot depend on others; we must go and stand
    alone.
Forward! — press right through between them — reckon
    afterward the cost —
Forward now, my soul, or never! Wait till day, and
    all is lost.

"Cuba libre! Cuba libre! Cuba libre!" came the
    cry.
Peace grew pale. War had awakened: and the morn-
    ing hopes were high.

   * Lee-bray.

"Cuba libre! Cuba libre!" Peace looked up—she
    could not speak.
Pity came and pointed seaward; and a tear crept
    down her cheek.
Far and black against the sunrise loomed the loaded
    convict ships
From the land of Hate and Avarice. Love came up
    with trembling lips.
Peace looked back; she saw them coming, Hope
    Triumphant in the lead,
Then came fixed Determination and the ragged hosts
    of Need.
Far behind hung shrewd Ambition, with his hireling
    band of brutes.
Duty hastened on without them, gathering up the late
    recruits.
On they came, and God was with them! Fear's own
    force took up the cry:
"Cuba libre! Cuba libre!" and the echoes made
    reply.
"Cuba libre! libre! libre!" Oh the hills did love
    the sound!
Peace herself rejoiced within her, and no longer
    looked around.
"Cuba libre!" clanged the anvils—she could hear
    them far and wide.
"Free ye Cuba!" swelled the answer down the long
    Atlantic side.
"Free ye Cuba—we are with you!" flashed the word
    from sea to sea—
"Banish Tyranny forever from the New World of the
    Free."

"Cuba libre! Cuba libre!" Happy they who loved
and heard;
Happy they who faced the world to spread and preach
the happy word ;
Happy they who hurried northward to supply who
stayed and fought;
Happy, happy they who helped them. Witness, ye
who helped them not.
Happy? Who had not been happy at the birth of
Freedom—say?
Is the black man sad and gloomy on Emancipation
Day?
Did the Signers toll the bells? Ah no. They rang
and rang on high,
Till the hills rejoice for ever on the Fourth Day of July.
And the sick man, the pale sick man, sweating on a
couch of pain,
He rejoiced those sounds, and smiling, drank them
deep, and harked again:
Raised his head from the hot pillow, listened to the
distant peals,
Crept up to the open window, and looked out across
the fields.
Oh the free fresh air of heaven, and the sweet smell of
the hay,
And the dreams of peace and quiet. He died happy
on that day.
"Independence! Independence!" screamed the
striplings in the streets.
Lofty little minds are awful when the bulging forehead
beats.

Mighty men were little children ; little children
    mighty men ;
And they marched out head to shoulder, to return no
    more again.
And the mothers, and the daughters, who were just as
    brave at home,
Toiling for the boys and fathers, who, alas, should
    never come.

"Gold or Silver !   Gold or Silver !" sped the madden-
    ing, magic word.—
"Gold or Silver ; which are you for?"   Sense was
    wounded when she heard.
"Gold or Silver for the masses—Gold or Silver for the
    rich—
Gold, or Gold, or Gold or Silver—Gold or Silver—
    which for which?"
"Gold or Silver !   Silver !   Silver !"   Agitators
    thronged the streets,
Damning all the rich together—even philanthropists
    were cheats.
Not a more offended people ever welcomed polling
    day,
When they too might give opinions in their own
    emphatic way.
"It's McKinley !" dinned the thousands in the mid-
    dle of the night.
"'Rah McKinley !" came the answer, "Courts are
    safe, and law is right !"
"'Rah McKinley !   'Rah McKinley !   Honor and
    Protection !   'Rah !

Down with loud Repudiation! Up with money and
the law!"
"Call Prosperity back from Europe, and shut out the
pauper breeds!
Build a wall against stagnation! Gold is what the
country needs."
"Gold? Where can the poor man get it? Poverty
earned what Luxury eats.
Progress waits upon Employment; and Employment
shuns the streets.
"They make money who have money to impose upon
the poor;
If the poor like men resent it, Wealth goes in and
shuts the door.
"Wealth will listen to no reasons, and will give no
reasons why.—
'Strike, and I will starve your families; you must
come to terms, not I.'"

Fruitless, fruitless, oh my brothers, is a warfare such
as this,
And the louder the complaining, wider yawns the
dark abyss.
Wider, deeper, more portentious grow the differences
of men;
While a kind, unselfish interest soon might heal them
up again.
Blindness to the ills of others makes our lot seem
worse than theirs:
Speak for Love; lead out with Virtue; look to God
and His affairs.

Listen: "Cuba! Cuba libre!" can ye hear above
    the moan?
Death and Famine drive them thither, gaunt,
    unfriended, and alone.
See them—women—little children—crawling on
    their hands and knees—
Rouse thee up, thou busy Business! Will you hear
    not even these?
Hunger! Oh thou hideous Hunger! Christ! are
    these the means of war?
Who will urge them back? What pretense? They
    shall see their homes no more.
Spain has starved their families. Heavens! ask me
    not what else they did.
God of Love have mercy on us—we who saw—Oh
    Christ forbid.
Feed the hungry, clothe the naked, help the helpless,
    rich or poor,
Worthy or unworthy—God knows; ours to keep, and
    His to cure.
Kind at home means constant kindness. Knaves may
    pass for saints abroad.
Deeds undone at home hang heavy on thy conscience
    and thy God.
Where are now the friends'they looked to? Who had
    thought a year ago
We, of all they put their trust in, would be first to
    say them no?
How much longer, ye wise statesmen, will ye blunder
    for the light?

Mottoes stamped on gold or silver will not bring the
    future right.
"God we trust."—but who shall serve Him? "God
    is Love."—and what are ye?
Brotherhood, not gold or silver, is the standard that
    must be.
Act! His hosts are marshaled, waiting. Act! The
    public voice is hoarse.
Who now wants investigation? Speak—and let your
    talk be terse.
Know ye not 't was our example,—that the sweet
    prospect that lured
Was the hope that they might some day, with the help
    that we assured,
Draw their little force together, just as we did ours,
    and hold
That the New World had decided to proceed without
    the Old?
Witness that the least among you, falsely in the
    Nation's name,
Sneered upon their lofty passions, and betrayed us to
    the blame.
God, have faith in us, Thy children, when we sneak
    from out Thy sight,
Bent on business of our own, when thine awaits us
    through the night.
Hear me! Hear me, ye great people! In the name
    of Christ the Son!
In the name of God our Father! this disgrace must
    not be done.

Loose on Spain the Yankee spirit—Gulf to Lakes, and
    West to East!
Peace, with all her hosts, is coming! Send for Bull,
    and set the feast!
Hear us! Cuba! Cuba libre! Independence now
    or death!
Force the pass! We come! we come! and all the
    angels hold their breath.

MARCH AND APRIL.

Loud, many-mooded March, with hurrying clouds,
Chill rains, cold, windy sunshine, and what not;
That strange, green, gaunt, outlandish month that
    crowds
His foolish days with one mad, freakish blot
Of births and deaths of flowers,—I know not what,—
The reckless boyhood of the year, in short,
Is past, and all his youthful sins forgot.
April, sweet month of first love, his consort,
Blooms in the blushing fields, and calls him from his
    sport.

MAY.

How cool you look this morning. Have you been
At Sabbath school? Where were you going now?
The last bell rang, and they were going in
As I came by. Don't go. Let me endow

Thy pure white corsage with this apple bough.
I cut it for thee coming o'er the hill.
Its blossoms are not lovelier than thou,
Sweet, fragrant flower.   Oh do you love me still,
When I am pale and thin?   You always, always
      will?

It is quite warm.   My heart beats so from running
Down the hillside, I scarce can do my best.
There,—is that right?   My fingers lose their
      cunning,
And modestly, so near thy fluttering breast,
Eager to pause, yet fearful to molest,
Quiver and halt, and halting, blush, and grow
Bewildered.
      Let us sit here, sweet, and rest.
No, dear, not tired exactly, but,—you know:
I dream of you all day.   The time seems very slow.

Ah, yes, a bright spring morning; but my sky
Sometimes will darken on such days as these.
Come to the orchard, and I'll tell you why;
I will feel better there among the trees.
My mind will feel the influence of the breeze,
And blossom into speech, if speech be true.
The man is moulded by the things he sees,
The air he breathes, the sounds he listens to.
If all we feel be God, so all we say and do.

Let us sit here.   First let me spread your cloak
On the thin grass, lest you take cold.   Ah me—

What an ideal spot beneath that oak.
And yet from there the house obscures the sea.
Let us stay here.   From this old apple tree
We have the ocean, and the ocean wall,
And the long curve of beach out in the bay,—
And a white sail, and the blue sky and all.
Beside, the blossoms here will touch us as they fall.

Now, dear, were I but master of the brush,
With genius in my soul, how might I rise,
Seize the occasion, catch the passing flush,
Enter and dwell where holy darkness lies
Deep in the dewy twilight of thine eyes,
Dwell and half dream,—dwell till the very paint
Wakes with a flush and throbs to realize
How 'neath my spell it breathes a living saint,
Clothed in an apple bough.

                    Reluctant, weak, and faint,
I feel myself emerging from a dream.
And my poor soul resumes me as of old,
But still exhausted, hates the things that seem,
And shuns to look, till by degrees, behold:
Whose lovely smile is this I see unfold?
My sweet Gertrude, my picture, oh my bride.
Will ever painter of an age of gold
Create a dream so pure and glorified
As thou, my promised love, in blossoms at my side?

With wasted eyes, and an ungifted arm,
How helpless were thy painter to enscroll

The modest beauty of thy face and form.
How weaker still thy poet to extol
The simple whiteness of so pure a soul.
'T were easier to invade the realms above,
Outsail the stars, and pass beyond control
Of God Himself, than in this flowery grove
Paint what no man can paint, a likeness of real
      love.

Serenely now the blossoms rise and fall
On their wide branches.   There is peace in them.
Were I this exile drooping on thy shawl,
Softly would I let go, waft from the stem,
And lodge upon the lace-embroidered hem,
So kindly, thou wouldst smile, and not protest.
As on the petal trembles the dew-gem,
So would I tremble on thy fragrant breast;
And if I fell, oh love,—take me, and let me rest.

Forgive me dear, I cannot sing; no use.
Who soar must fall; and those who venture high,
God help them when the excitement cuts them loose,
And they come gasping headlong through the sky.
Who talk the most say least, sometimes, and I,
Feeling my failure, like a little child
Must feign to laugh, lest I break down and cry,
So sensitive am I, my songs so wild,
I and my best attempts must die unreconciled.

Yet I have felt all earthly discontent
Vanish away, when with one high endeavor,

Seizing the stillness, I have given vent
To words that chilled my being to deliver.
Sweet, living truth, direct from God the Giver,
Wholesome with consolation,—His, not mine.
My words will fail, but God's live on forever.
Oh let me live in one exalted line,
While volumes past me crowd to prosperous decline.

A man of moods? No, boy. Boy to the letter.
The rest is true. I glory in the truth.
Let the world laugh, they cannot make me bit-
    ter ;
I go to meet them, not with nail and tooth,
I hail them with the confidence of youth ;
Weigh with them kindly ; make them all my
    friends ;
And find them fond and human, not uncouth,
Willing ofttimes to sympathize my ends,
Whereas I might have thought them enemies, and
    fiends.

I love all men when God is in my heart.
Would I could always think to keep Him there.
He tells me these crude souls are but a part
Of the kind scheme He has,—that everywhere
Each of His children may work out some share
Toward the great day that He alone can see.
He speaks ; and in that instant I prepare
To do His will, wherever that may be,—
Face the dark night with joy, and He goes out with
    me.

Oh, and what rapture, — what heroic, high,
Unnamable felicity exalts
The soul that harkens, goes, nor questions why,
Into the mine of hopeless night, nor halts
To pick the wreckage from the sea of faults,
But with a faith that loves the wind, and hears
The approving voice of God, goes and assaults
In His high name the thieves of human tears,
And lifts them up with love, and whispers in their ears.

All men have tasted of these joys, Gertrude,
For men may rise above themselves at times.
Even kings have yielded to the timely mood,
And made propitiation for their crimes.
And poets, who have revelled in dull rhymes
Of sad licentiousness, have been inspired
From their last state to ring the heavenly chimes
To such high flights that angels have admired.
But ah, their strength was gone ; alas, how soon they
    tired.

Yet none can touch celestial solitudes,
And can we wonder that the sensitive poet,
Descending from these strange, unearthly moods,
Feels he has failed, and trembles lest we know it ?
He aimed beyond us, but fell far below it,
Else his high flight had past all comprehension.
Just as the heart is touched the eyes will show it.
There is no sweeter praise than rapt attention.
Moved or unmoved, our duty is to hear;
Art asks no higher tribute than a look, a smile, a tear.

My friend is gentle master of my heart.
Not flatterer; no, nor critic; but his word
Is caught with rapture, and preserved in art;
He lives forever, and the souls he stirred
Shall rise to bless him and themselves be heard.
There is no end to kindness, once it lives.
Shall we forget who loved us when we erred?
God bless the rare old friendship that forgives;
The heart with two big hands, that welcomes, and
      believes.

Next to the man men love the poet.   Byron,
With all his littleness, was a mightier power
Than any king whose bloody rod of iron
Smote the weak times and bade the nations cower.
Did not great David in an awful hour
Sin against God, Whom he was sent to sing?
And who will say he was not still the flower
Of all the ancients, warrior, bard or king,
That down to us with awe the solemn Scriptures
      bring?

Mistake me not, O Gertrude; none can know
Better than thou what I do think of sin.
Ask God how from polluted sources flow
The streams of life that we refresh us in.
I think how handicapped some men begin,
And wonder what had come of me if I,
Born with such fire, humored as they have been,
Had met these same enticements I defy.

The mighty weak, like shields before the times,
Stand out and take the blame for all the common
    crimes.

What man knows of himself, if for some cause
He had been born with passions and weak will?
And Burns,—had he but met the right applause,
Would he have been the loud exciseman still?
God had His purpose in each: we may kill,
Drug with false praise, or starve into dejection,
But he will send another to fulfill
His high design, and point us to perfection.
Happy the man, and perfect in God's eyes,
Who, though he fall, and fall, and fall again, still
    tries.

Yet there are some with superstitious notions
Who will not pause, but organize to fight
Imaginary devils with emotions
That warp their minds and dim their spiritual sight;
Till, losing charity, they lose the light;
And from their piteous darkness you may hear them
Calling their man-made God of wrath and spite
To judge the wicked world, while ever near them,
An all-forgiving Father grieves that his children fear
    Him.

Many with satisfaction wait the day
When wholesale justice shall condemn the risen,
Happy, poor souls, that God shall not delay
To cast His enemies in eternal prison.

Such are the minds that count it sin to reason.
But God loves them, and waits. He loved the Jews
From whose dead errors works this sacred poison,
That we, three thousand years towards Heaven,
     must choose,
Or be despised of men who hold these morbid views.

Oh that all nations knew that God is Love,
And recognized in Christ the gentle Brother.
Jesus, (and Washington,) ordained above,
And many a man is of a holy mother.
All are the children of the one kind Father,
Jesus the only worthy of us all;
Who teaches us to live for one another,
Lest by one's selfishness another fall.
And that is all there is. The task is very small.

Father, direct us to avoid the snares
And gloomy pitfalls of theology.
Teach us how sweeter praises are than prayers,
Thanksgiving than beseeching,—let us be
Grateful and glad, resigning all to Thee,
Who in Thy goodness cannot humor men
And still be wise of what they cannot see.
Teach us to know our duty, not to scan
Thee, whom we cannot know, trusting until we can.

When from our joys we turn to bear the trials
That make us men, prepared for greater joys,
Fill Thou our souls, that we may keep the smiles
Of happy peace for timely counterpoise.

Ashes of Roses

So shall we go about with little noise;
And in our hearts, not in our mouths, shall lie
The faith good wisdom welcomes and employs.
Thou sparest none from kindness, all must die.
Oh may we love Thee more, and come without a sigh.

Alas, and oh alas, that men should stoop
To the calm bartering of their souls for praise.
Alas that I have been the easy dupe
Of vulgar plaudits in my earlier days.
Woe is the bard whose eagerness for the bays
Persuades his holy office to receive
The gorgeous wreath that withers and decays.
Woe is the man who has no more to leave
Than odes to wasted time, and deeds beyond retrieve.

I falter, dear, for I, young though I am,
Have juggled time and talent for applause;
Till, grown to be the shadow of my sham,
I took delight in building fame of straws,
If for no other reason than because.
But winter came, and these successive snows
Have kept me so employed that now I pause
And find myself companion of the rose.
Love, in thy modest eyes my real ambition glows.

I think of thee, and I am seized to paint
The truth, far in the future, and I cast
Check to the winds, and leave old dull Restraint
Gaping at me from out the wasted past,
And startled Time, bewildered, stands aghast.

I heed them not. I only throb within
And speed the swifter, lest the fire outlast
The nervous fuel ere the work begin—
If I can save my strength for the finish I will win.

Why should I win?   What man enjoys his prize
As much as he who lost it envies him?
A heavy name is greater in some eyes
Than modest faithfulness.   Each has his whim.
And gratified, it suddenly grows dim
And worthless.   Yet the man who toils ahead
Scorns a reward for duty; and his hymn
Swells to the skies, though from a shivering bed
He goeth forth at dawn, unfriended, and unfed.

Come, dear, let us go in; perhaps a song
Would brighten me a little, for I fear
A transient ray of sunshine will not long
Keep back the clouds that seem to disappear.
Oh would my soul were like the mountaineer,
Who sees the clouds beneath him, while above
He looks into a sky forever clear.
The eagle is his symbol, mine the dove;
Heroic war his song, mine love, eternal love.

Yes, God is Love.   You know just what to say
To light me through the clouds.   Come, let us sing.
I'm glad I left my harp here yesterday.
I'll tune it while you go upstairs and bring
Your violin.   Hark, how the echoes ring
Through the still house, to the most breathful touch.

Don't be gone long.
                    Oh is there anything
In this wide world that I do love as much
As the sweet smile of willingness.   I will hum
A low, wierd interlude, and harken till she come.

Hush!
The world is gone.
Alone,
Alone,
Far out upon
The farthest zone
Of space
I, Music,
Sit listening.
Hush:

Hush:
Nothing but silence.
Nothing but night.
No stir,
No light,
Nothing.
The things that were
Are dead.
Darkness instead,
And blur.
The expectant void
Sways and vibrates
With worlds unborn.
How long,

Ashes of Roses

How long till morn?
Wait.
God waits.
And I,
I, Music, wait
And palpitate,
Stirred,
But unheard.

Listen!
Hark!
The birth of sound!
I feel!
I hear!
Oh strings, resound!
Fly!—fly! O Fear,
And thou, O Space,
Give place!
Hail!

Strike! Oh ye strings,
Rejoice!
Rejoice!
Creation brings
Her mighty voice,
All living things
And rocks and springs
Call to the day
"Rejoice!
"Rejoice!"
Hark .

Ashes 𝔬𝔣 Roses

Far away
Faint Echo sings
"Rejoice!
"Rejoice!
"Rejoice!"
And dies
Along the skies
Where Quiet lies
Sleeping.
Hush.

Nothing but just a little offhand song
To amuse my spirits with till your return.
It had been shorter, but you staid so long
I let the lamp of inspiration burn,
Spread the wide wings of lofty unconcern,
And in that instant was beyond all thought,
Save that unconsciously I harked to learn
When you were coming, till each sound I caught
Impulsed me on to reach almost the heights I sought.

And I had reached it, but as you came nearer
The inspiration blushed, and ran and hid.
Or else I blushed; for when I have a hearer
I always do.   That is, I always did.
And that I lose my deference God forbid.
There is a joy in modesty of soul.
We watch it in the patient invalid
With tears of hope.   And who would set control
Above his gentler self, and bravely spoil the whole?

Would I could be what I admire in men.
Would I were great, even to the highest flush
Of young ambition. Yet the voice, the pen,
Are less than simple goodness, and I blush.

The organist in the dim cathedral's hush
Looks through the darkness, and his fingers feel
Along the breathless keys with tremulous touch,
And on his listening soul, faint, but how real,
Far through the holy night the heavenly answers
    steal.

He hears. He answers. With emotion clinging
To the low flute that mellows through the gloom,
He hears the angels answer,—hears them singing,—
And now the silence whispers "Hark! they come!"
"Hark! hark!" the organ echoes, "hark! be
    dumb!"
And in the hush that follows you can hear
The labored breathing of great pipes, and some
Groan their impatience to the organeer,
Who lingers listening still. But see—strange lights
    appear:

And he can tell the voices that come first;
Hears the great masters leading; and with zeal
Opens the throbbing pipes that else had burst,
Lets out his soul and echoes peal on peal.
Loud from the lofty pipes the raptures reel,
Harmoniously confounded. Far below,

Ashes of Roses

The heaving pedals tremble to reveal
That depth of joy the deep alone can know,
And the great lofts reply, like seas that ebb and
  flow.

Now the high notes like flames of moving fire
Above the rolling clouds of joyful bass,
Leap from the thousand throats of crypt, dome,
    spire,
And flash tuned lightning up through thundering
    space.
Hark the far anthems of the populace:
The excited chimes, the sacred iron bell,
And the great organ gladdens on apace,
And the walls rumble with the mighty swell—
Music and Madness wed—and roaring wind, and
    hail.

As when a spark of its own ardor glows
In the dead solstice of a summer night,
Feeds to a flame, and brightens as it grows,
Till sea and city, stars, clouds, mountain height
Peer from the flickering darkness pale with fright,
Then as they catch the excitement and join in,
And the big ocean trembles with delight,
The opposite foothills echoing to the din
Of voices, that like angels all in white
Move slowly singing up the mountain side
"Glory to Him Who lives! We come! Behold our
    pride."

Just as triumphant inspiration comes
To that high climax of the mighty scale
Where blare of golden horns, and metal drums,
Are heard no more above the nightingale,
And delicate Music feels her lips grow pale
And tremble, and she finds herself alone
Far in the midst of silence, then there fail
The slow-returning choirs, until the tone
Is lost among the stars, that roll about the throne.

MIDSUMMER NIGHT.

The sun is low in the woods;
  And the long, twilight shadows are creeping
    Over the lily-pond, solemn and still,
Where the odor of hay floats by,
  And the reapers are through with their reaping,
    And the bullfrogs down in the lily-pond
    Croak, while the little ones shrill.

Let us drift with the breeze, Oh love,
  Like a shadow a-creeping, a-creeping,
    Over the lily-pond, close by the mill;
Where the white swans dream and float,
  And ever the willows are weeping,
    And their images down in the lily-pond
    Touch them, and quiver, and thrill.

Let us drift with the breeze, Oh love,
  Like a shadow a-creeping, a-creeping,

Over the lily-pond, under the hill;
Where the clover droops from the bank,
  And the cattle are dozing and sleeping,
    And the stars, deep down in the lily-pond,
    Watch us, and tremble, and thrill.

POOR.

We're goin' away to-morrow day,
  Down to ne railroad crack,
An' goin' on ne choo-choo cars,
An' tooken ever'fing nat's ars,
  An' never comin' back.

My papa's got a whole big lots
  A-jobs, way to a place
Where th' ain't no peoples 'cep' but us,
An' mans nat grives ne omblibus,
  An' whiskers on the'r face.

It's way, way past ne woods somewheres.
  My papa knows.   He's been.
An' mamma says they's ugly scares,
An' wild In-dins, an' snakes, an' bears,
  An' all kinds a-fings fwif skin.

My papa says we're poor, an' he
  Can't git work here to do.

Wisht I wuz rich, an' mamma an' me,
An' papa, an' gramma, too, all three,
An' sister, an' us, why nen, why we,
  Why we'd be rich, like you.

An' we'd have pie, an' cake, an' sweet,
  An' butter on ar bread,
An' m'lasses, too, an' steak, an' meat,
An' oh, iss ever-fing to eat.
  Nen wouldn' I be glad?

THE COUNTY FAIR.

One time I seen a bray-big b'loon!
Fourf-a-July af'ernoon,
Guess it wuz, er to ne Fair.
I donno—I guess nat's where,
'Cause my bray-big brover Ed
Runned away f'om me, he did,
An' slipped away somewheres an' hide.
Nen I iss runned an' cried an' cried.
Nen he comed an' said 'at he
Done it fer to iss scare me.
Nen we're went where's krees an' fings,
An' birds in 'um what they're sings;
Only they nain't nany, 'cause
When I peeped up where they wuz,
Why they wuzn't nany nere;
Way out to ne Coundy Fair.

Ed he ketched a bray-big snake!
An' killed its head off fwif a rake!
An' lots a-min they 're comed an' said
"How-do" to my brover Ed.
Nen Ed, why he taked holt my hand,
An' we're iss runned where they 's a band.
An' bray-big race crack, mile around!
An' horses scootin' round an' round
All ne time!   An' bell to ring,
An' make 'um go, an' ever'fing,
An' p'leece to keep ne peoples back,—
Only we 're skipped acrosst ne crack
When they're wuzn't lookin' nen,
'Cause Ed he knowed the p'leece, I b'leeve,
'Cause he called one "Hello, ol' man!"
An' laffed, an' taked a-holt his sleeve.
An' 'nover p'leece comed up to Ed,
An' I fergit whut all he said,
Only he laffed an' looked at me,
An' hold me up so I could see
Way crosst ne ring! an see a horse
Iss runnin', an' a nover horse
Iss tryin' to ketch up, an' couldn't,
An' nover horses tried, an' couldn't,
An' I iss hollered down to Ed,
An' nen he taked me, 'cause he said
The p'leeceman hat to went on ne crack
An' keep ne res' ne peoples back.
An' nen here comed a nigger-man
Iss scootin' past as fas' he can
On top a horse, an' shake his whip,

An' hollerin' "Git ep! git ep!"
An' nen some more comed scootin' past,
An' they're was iss goin' awful fast,
An' novern comed, an' when ne crowd
Wasn' lookin' I hollered wight out loud.

An' nen I seen some pigs, an' cows,
An' bulls, an' horses, an' dray-big sows,
An' cutest littie pigs, an' sheeps,
An' papa sheeps, an' mamma sheeps
An' loculmodives runnin' round,
Fwifout no cracks! wight on ne ground!
An' big win'meels, an' water come,
An' didn' haf to pump atall.
An' Ed he went an' got me some.
An' candy, too.   I guess nat's all.
An' they wuz ever'body nere,
Way out to ne Coundy Fair.

Oh yes!   I seen a bray-big b'loon!
An' big clo'es-basket, an' some min
Comed along an' iss got in!
Nen ever'body hollered!
'Cause nen ne b'loon
Iss got away, an' went skrait up!
An' peoples hollered, an' it wouldn' stop!
An' nen ne min slung lots a-sand
Out a-bags, an' waved the'r hand!
Nen ever'body hollered nen,
An' wathed the'r han'kercheefs again,
An' I telled Ed whut wuz they doin'?

An' he says, "You're'll see perty soon."
An' nen I wait, an' by an' by,
When they 're git up past ne sky
Ne b'loon iss upset, perty nigh.
Nen Ed he seen it, an' some min,
They 're seen it, an' some nover min,
They 're seen it, an' I couldn' see it.
An' whole lots a-ladies couldn' see it.
An' nen, why nen, why Ed he says,
"I guess that mus' be all they is."
An' nen I tooked a-holt his hand,
An' we 're went wight past nover band.
An' nen I got to went an' go
Past where they wuz a big side-show,
An' min a-hollerin', an' nen us
An' Ed got in a nomblibus,
An' took us skrait down town fer nickle.
An' I went to sleep, an' Ed hat to tickle
Me an' nover little boy.
An' I di'n't know ne little boy.
Only Ed, he knowed ne little boy.
An' I wuz to ne Coundy Fair.
I bet you wisht nat you wuz nare.

THE CALFIE-COW.

Wunst, a 'ittol caffie-cow
  Lost its ma, one day,
An' couldn' find her, nanyhow,
  Nen iss runned an' say :
    "Ma! Ma! Ma!" iss nat way.

An' nen her mamma comed along
  F'om where her start to go,
An' ast her what on earf was wrong
  'At maked her holler so.
"Moo! Moo! Moo!"
  Nat's all I know.

THE STREAM.

The brooklet runs to meet the brook
  The brook to meet the river;
The river flows to join the sea,
  And lose itself forever.

My childhood babbled into youth;
  Now youth, through manhood driven,
Will leave me soon below the falls,
  In placid view of Heaven.

Choose well thy course,—keep pure, my soul,
  And oh where'er thy duty,
Reflect thy God before all men,
  Though few admire thy beauty.

So shalt thou flow a perfect stream,
  Lost in His love forever;
And men shall say, "How sweet to stray
  Beside this ancient river."

MY TOWN.

You may go the world up and down,
　And many a town you'll see,
But there's no town like my town,
　No difference how poor it be.
For there are the dear old friends
　Who knew me when I was a boy.
Bless their kind hearts, it sends
　A thrill of the wholesomest joy
To land in town and go up the street,
Welcomed by all the people I meet.
Oh the poorest town is hard to beat
　For the boy who was born and raised there.

You may hold to it up and down
　That yours is the finest to see,
But it's no town like my town,
　No difference how fine it be.
For there are the people that stare,
　And wonder who that fellow is.
Bless their hearts though, I declare,
　It's human to wonder and quiz.
And those same cold strangers, that only seem so,
Are kind old friends of yours, I know.
Oh the coldest town will overflow
　To the boy who was born and raised there.

But ah, when these friends are gone,
　Gone, all but you and me,
Not your town nor my town
　Will be what it used to be.

167

We'll miss the kind faces we knew,
  And forget the old honest pride,
And we'll argue, as old men do,
  That the world has grown too wide.
But God has arranged for the dear old men
To meet together as boys again,
And we'll go and leave the old towns then
  To the boys who were born and raised there.

THE PIGGIES.

Five little pigs came in our yard.
  Heigh-ho little piggie-wiggies!
And they went to rooting without regard.
  Hey there! little piggie-wiggies.
I didn't like to go out in the rain,
But they went on rooting with might and main.
My wife just tapped on the window-pane.
  Ho-ho! little piggie-wiggies!

We had to laugh when they looked around,
  Ha-ha! little piggie-wiggies!
With their little bright eyes all covered with ground.
  Tut, tut, little piggie-wiggies.
We tapped again, and they wheeled about
On their short fat legs and scampered out,
And each made a nose at us with his snout.
  Why, why, little piggie-wiggies.

THE MOLE.

Look, love, at the pretty mole I found.
I saw it going into the ground,
And caught it, and brought it home to you.
I was just coming out of the field where I husk,
When the moon peeped over the Indian mound,
And I saw something crossing the road in the dusk.
I knew what it was ; and before I could pause,
Boy-like, I had him, body and claws,
And was hurrying home with my prize to you.
I thought at first how nice it would look
To make you a dainty money-book
Of the delicate fur, but my heart was true,
And I said "No, Paul, that will never do.
God is merciful, we must be."
But I brought it home for you to see.
Isn't it fat?   Just come and feel.
Its fur is as soft as the softest seal.
What a strange blue cast—Oh hear him squeal !
Get me the cage, dear.   Poor little mole,
Did I hurt you?   There, now, open the hole,
And I 'll drop him in.   He can't get out.
See him poke through the cracks with his pointed
          snout.
What a comical face he has when he pries
With his broad, thick hands, and his wee, bead eyes.
Whoa, there, get down, little mole,—you 'll fall.
Look out ! I 'm sorry.   It hurt, I know.
Little people were only made to crawl,
And should be quite careful how high they go.

Just like a boy, though,—at it again.
But the stubbornest boys make the best of men ;
And a few hard bumps are good at the start;
Go it, young wilful, and keep good heart.
Come, love, he is angry now, for they say
Moles are cross little things that way.
And we'd be, too, if we lived in the sod,
Shut off from the beautiful world of God.
I pity a mole, as I pity all those
Who survey the world's end at the tip of their nose,
And never look up at the far blue sky,
And forget their vexations, as you and I.
Yet maybe I wrong this poor little mole.
Birds hymn their Creator, and why not he?
It was preached that the black man had no soul,
But a kind old sinner set them free,
And now they're God's children the same as we.
Who knows? When I seized my little slave
He was probably out for his modest share
Of the autumn harvest our Father gave.
For industry reaps the rewards of prayer,
And all is for all, whether mole or man,
At it early, and get what we can,
At it together, and praise the Lord,
Remember the poor, and forget the reward.

But supper is ready and waiting I see.
Oh dear little wife, you are so good to me.
Come, let us sit down in the presence of Him
Who was always our Guest when the days were
　　dim,

But Who is our bountiful Host to-night.
I remember you told me 't would all come right.
God bless you, sweet Gertrude. What would I do
In this beautiful world, were it not for you?

But this little mole is on my mind.
It is never right to be unkind.
I am sorry. I wish I had let it go.
It hurts me to see it worried so.
Yet how should we love these queer little elves,
If we didn't catch one and see for ourselves?
Hereafter, when I see one burrow down
Into his subterranean halls,
Arching the sod, and dividing the walls,
As he makes his way to the fairy town
With stolen goodies for the babies that wait
With mamma mole, at the city gate,
I 'll laugh to myself, and hurry on,
So he 'll come for more when I am gone.
Now, to-night, when the moon is high, and we take
Our usual walk, overlooking the lake,
We 'll carry our little prisoner back,
With some corn for him in a paper sack.

TO KEATS, AFTER READING HIS LIFE.

Thus ends the tale. And it is long since then.
　But beauty lives, and life is lovelier now.
　Oh had they known thee as we know thee now,
Perhaps they had received thee kindlier then.

But poetry is still crime with average men,
   And commonness is as hateful to the brow
   Of delicate thought as 't was the days when thou,
Sweet, gentle boy, didst weep, and sing again.
But patient wisdom sees a better age,
   Far through the trying years, when great-grown
         man
      Shall value greatness ; and the still, high courts
Of listening and attention shall engage
   To hear from bards who at thy feet began,
      That beauty still is truth by all reports.

MARRIAGE.

It is my sweetest blessing now
   That I may re-begin
With one who sees before I point,
   And can be trusted in.

Who feels before I speak ; who knows
   More truth than I can tell ;
Who, though my language poorly flows,
   Will understand as well.

And yet for whom my thoughts consume
   The simple words I use,
That flame to just the glow I seek,
   Ere I have power to choose.

Ashes of Roses

Whose speech is music, and whose hush
  Is the long, modest pause
That starts in tune with gentle blush,
  Too sweet for strange applause.

Who lives for me, that I may live
  For Him Who gave our life
To be a mild demonstrative
  Of happy man and wife.

Gertrude, my precious, perfect me,
  Made delicate and pure,
Thou more than I can hope to be,
  Though I may long endure,

My soul, unlike me as I am,
  But all I should have been,
Whose symbol is the little lamb,
  That has no thought of sin.

Yet in thy time thou shalt be more
  Than thou thyself art now,
To draw me upward as before,
  As none else knoweth how.

Just as we help ourselves the most,
  By helping others first,
That difference cannot be lost
  Till all sin be dispersed.

Go on, my soul, my sweeter soul,
  And lead me to the skies;
There where the years forever roll,
  And marriage never dies,

There where the truth shall all be known,
  That no one knoweth now,
We go, sweetheart, but not alone,
  For God shall teach us how.

FAILURE.

Far in the past's eternal afterglow
  Celestial glory gilds the silent west.
The darkness gathers round me as I go;
  Sing on, my soul, remember, there is rest.
The glow will fade, the day will soon be past;
  The night will come, and listening, mock thy steps;
But thou be great; the time will come at last
  When men shall love thee, though it be, perhaps,
  When thou hast dropped behind the world's elapse
In silence. Would that I could always dwell
  In the calm quiet of unruffled thought;
And sing for those about me, and could tell
Of the far ages that I see so well,
  When men shall love each other, as they ought.

LAST NIGHT.

Last night, when I awoke, the frozen winds
  In mad pursuit of space were sallying forth

Out of the forests to the west and north,
    Slamming the doors and howling through the rooms,
Banging the gates, and sweeping on like fiends
    Across the fields, and on into the glooms.
And ever one was left to grope about
    Sighing, far in a lone room.   I could not sleep.
I closed the windows down, and still without,
    The crazy gates did rattle, and moan, and weep,
      And I was shut within the house alone.
And a quick sadness seized me, and I felt
    For thy face, love, remembering thou wert gone
    Down to the river, in the cozy town,
To visit thy good mother where she dwelt.

LITTLE ALLEGRA.

To-day I got a valentine
    From my sweet little cousin.
Before I was a married man
    I used to get a dozen.

But since a pretty school girl stands
    Beside me, to protect me,
My little kindergarten friends
    Have purposed to neglect me.

However, we shall not despair
    While skies are blue above us,
And little Allegra shall swear
    By all the stars to love us.

CHICKENOLOGY.

I.

All ar hens walks on the'r han's,
  'Cause the'r han's is same as feet.
An' ar ol' roosters, they're iss stan's,
  An' crows, an' crows, an' eat an' eat.
My mamma says that there's because
That's how chickuns always does.

II.

Yes, an' when ar big hens sets,
  They're hatches little chicks, like ars.
An' mamma says, when the big sun sets,
  It hatches little stars.

III.

My U'cle Ben says,
  Ef I c'lect hens' teef,
He'll gi' me dollar
  Fer ever' one.
We're got a ol' hen
  Nat's pit-nigh deef,
An' can't hartly swaller,
  'N'am go' to git a gun,
An' shoot its neck off,
  An' git a dollar,
An' buy some candy.
  Nen won't I holler?

176

TO MYSELF.

Do now, to-day, all that you know you ought.
No generous effort ever came to nought.
Work.   For the night will come when they must
      work
Who, through the day, permit themselves to shirk.
And they who did their best, though they need rest,
Must stay and help while they have strength to stand.
So shall the work be finished in the end.

TO MY BROTHER ARTHUR.

Once, at the long farewell of day,
   Above the wide-mouthed river,
I took my contemplative way
   Where the golden waters quiver.
Unmarked of men, the same as they,
   Heirs of the great forever.

Now, like an idle ship that's furled,
   I watched the ships at sea;
Or where the rolling breakers curled,
   And splashed the beach with spray.
I was at peace with all the world,
   The world at peace with me.

And then I met a thoughtful man.
   (Ah, there are too few such.)
And, glad to meet him, thus began :
   (Respectful was my touch.)

"I am a boy, but I enjoy
  Good company very much."

"I hope you find enough," he said.
  I answered, "Yes, indeed.
The world is full of books unread,
  That every boy should read;
And now and then I ply the pen,
  For practice, which I need."

"Why practice with the pen, young man?
  The world has books enough.
You said yourself that every shelf
  Was loaded with such stuff.
You'll starve to death." I held my breath.
  His way was rather rough.

I was too quick. "I'd rather starve,"
  I said, "than not stand true
To Him Who has His hopes set high
  On everything I do."
"You're young," he said, and turned his head.
  He hurt me through and through.
I did not have the heart to brave
  Against such interview.

With quivering lips I thanked him well.
  He answered not a word.
How I moved on I cannot tell.
  Oh, it was very hard,

To think a fellow-man would kill
  My hopes, without regard.

I looked beyond the glowing sky,
  And found my comfort there.
And though a tear stood in my eye,
  I soon forgot my care,
And pitied him whose soul was dim,
  And took him in my prayer.

That night I rose and took my hat
  And sought the river side.
The night was dark, and not a spark
  Showed where the waters glide.
I was the only one to hark
  The lapping of the tide.

I wrote; and though I could not see,
  I loved what I did write;
And while I wrote, it seemed to me,
  The paper blazed with light;
I looked: the moon had burst its noon;
  The clouds were fleecy white.

And Arthur, many a time since then,
  Though wounded to the core,
Have I found solace through my pen,
  Forgiving, as before.
And though the same should strike again,
  I'll love him more and more.

LITTLE BIRDS.

A little brown bird sat in our tree,
      Singing.
A little brown bird in a very big tree,   ~
And he stopped and said "Howd'e do" to me
      And went on singing.

I recognized him as soon as he spoke,
      Singing.
He looked like his little old kinfolk
That used to live in our big oak,
      Singing and singing.

A little brown birdie beneath him sat,
      Listening.
And when she saw me she turned like that!
And asked him whom was I looking at,
      Staring and listening.

I let on like I never heard,
      Listening.
Then she said "This is getting too absurd.
It's too public a place for a little girl bird,
      And people listening."

I heard him then, as I slipped away,
      Whispering.
I hope he'll coax her and get her to stay,
Don't you? Then I'll climb up some day,
      Peeping, and whispering,

And then I 'll hurry down to you,
    Whispering,
And then I 'll put the big ladder through,
And you can climb up and peep in too,
    Laughing, and whispering.

WHEN WE WERE MARRIED.

The woods were full of flowers, love,
    When I came by to-day ;
In just a few short hours, love,
    'T will be the first of May.
And then in one sweet month, love,
    And it will be a year
Since you and I were married, love,
    And are you happy, dear?

Oh are you happy, happy, dear?
    And do I make you glad?
And do you never, never dream
    Of the joys you might have had?
And do you love me, love me, dear,
    As you did that happy morn,
When you and I were married, dear,
    And I was weak and worn ?

Oh the woods were full of flowers, love,
    When I came by to-day.
I have counted all the hours, love,
    Since you were called away.

And I thought in one day more, love,
And I would see you here,
A week since we were parted, love,
And are you happy, dear?

Oh we are happy, happy, dear,
For God hath made us glad;
And we shall never, never dream
Of the joys we might have had.
Oh let us love and thank Him, dear,
As we did that happy morn,
When you and I were married, dear,
And I was weak and worn.

AFTER HEARING A FAMOUS EVANGELIST.

God is my Father, and I knew Him not.
But he knew me, and loved me, and was patient.
Ye joyful, preach; but be not rash; be patient.
These are His own; and have ye too forgot?
I understand them best; they cannot see.
Oh let me love them; leave them here with me.
Urge not thy superstitions. Are ye God,
That threat mankind with vengeance, and the
grave?
Man gives no time to love that will not save
For its own sake, whose gospel is the rod.
He faces judgment and the eternal wrath
Unflinching; for he knows he cannot die.

He feels God stir within him, and he hath
   A silence for all creeds.   For by and by
Truth shall transcend the church.   The day will come
   When God shall be no more misunderstood.
   The error robs the truth of half its good.
We are inspired, and shall our lips be dumb?
Till then I shall still hear you and receive
   Error with truth ; for I have much to learn,
Much to endure, many to believe,
   Ere I am calm, and ready for my turn.

TO MY BROTHER ARTHUR, EMBARKING
FOR CUBA.

   The breeze was at our back,
     And the shades of our sails before,
   And over the water spread the track
     To the sands of our native shore.

   Over the waters gleamed the way
     In the glow of the sinking sun,
   And the billows rolled like liquid gold
     Till the starry night came on.

   And into the starry, chilly night,
     And over the sighing swell,
   With here and there a gleam of light,
     And now and then a bell.

Till the stumbling seas on hands and knees
  Groped after us in the dark,—
It is a lonely joy at sea
  To lean on the rail and hark.

But ah, look up at the silent worlds,
  That roll through the awful deep,
And think how far through the night they are,
Star and planet, and planet and star,
  Rolling and never asleep.

Oh brother of mine, may peace be thine
  When out on the flying foam
Thou turnest from all the stars that shine,
  To think of the ones at home.

For there is a sorrow above all pain,
  That binds us to those we love,
And a peace that no man can explain,
If we but remember whose hands contain
  The sea, and the stars above.

TO LAIRD EASTON.

Lythe is the willow withe;
  But my love is more graceful to me.
Fair is the Venus of myth;
  But my love is far fairer than she.
The little girl with the rose in her hair.
Show me one that is half so fair.

Ashes of Roses

Cool is the early morn,
    When the dew is wet on the grass;
Green are the fields of corn,
    That rustle us as we pass.
And when our work in the garden is done,
Calm is the glow of the setting sun.

We love, and gather our feast,
    All in the still twilight;
Then in the quiet east
    We watch the glories of night,
Till the fields are lost, and the woods grow deep,
And all but the stars are gone to sleep.

Who is as happy as we?
    'T is noble to toil with the hands.
And God hath given to me
    A woman, who understands.
The little girl with the rose in her hair.
Oh there is none that is half so fair.

Cherries are on our shelves,
    Strawberries, and everything good.
We picked them and canned them ourselves;
    My little girl understood.
But summer is long, and there 's much to do.
Our trees are drooping with peaches, too.

Come when the year sits down,
    And smiles at the goodness of God;

When the fruits are yellow and brown,
  And the graceful goldenrod
Sways and dies by the roadside fence,
And summer is gone, and the rains commence.

Then indoors by the glow
  Of the warm fire, watching the blaze,
We talk of the long ago,
  And plan for the winter days;
And the good we hope to do when we can,
When she is a woman, and I am a man.

Come when the still frost cracks
  In the winter solitudes;
Then with bright steel saw and axe
  We go to the echoing woods.
And her voice rings out from tree to tree—
She is gathering nuts, and is calling me.

I come. She is beautiful, Laird.
  I know I am manly and rough,
But we are so happily paired,
  I cannot love her enough.
God bless her and keep her till I am old.
Yet for His sake we could brave the cold.

Thoughts of death, like a cloud,
  Pass over the winter sun,—
But she calls my name aloud:
  And I see a rabbit run!

Ashes of Roses

And her happy eyes have a kindly tear
For the joy of loving and being here.

We understand, and are glad.
　She piles up the hickory bark,
And I dream of the day we were wed.
　She is singing.　The angels hark:
And I feel a thrill to the steps of Heaven !
Oh Lord, what have I not been given.

Hush : in the solemn awe
　Of the great cathedral oaks,
Comes the delicate sing of the saw,
　Or the loud, re-echoing strokes ;
And the odor of chips is the incense there
That God detects in our busy prayer.

So in the frosty morn,
　Till the low sun smiles at noon,
And the steam is slow upborne
　From the glades that were green in June ;
And tired, and hungry, and full of love,
We gather our things, and prepare to move.

Some day I'll come again,
　With a neighbor's boy and team,
And the twigs will snap, and the chain
　Will rattle against the beam,
And the loading will sound through the startled woods
And waken the owl where she shivers and broods.

Ashes o' Roses

Now on the old rail fence
  We linger, and rest awhile.
She is tired.   My inner sense
  Can see it beneath her smile.
Loaded down with bundles of wood,
I cannot help her.   I wish I could.

Across the thawing fields,
  Slowly we toil apace.
She flags, but she never yields,—
  I watch her beautiful face,
And my anxious heart forgets the weight
Of the bundles of bark, as I watch my mate.

Now she is ahead of me,
  Against the cold, gray sky.
It must be a picture to see,
  My little plain wife and I,
She with the heavy, shouldered axe,
I laboring steadily in her tracks.

After our simple meal
  We sit by the kitchen fire,
At home!   But I curb my zeal,
  And cease, for fear you will tire.
I quite forgot it was warm July.
The clouds are magnificently high.

Come, little girl, let us go.
  (She's been sitting here in the shade,

Sewing; and you shall know
What dear little things she has made.
Wait. Not now. We'll be happier soon.
Come study with us this afternoon.

(Dear are the books we read;
Instruction is all we seek.
Many the things we need,—
But look at the glow on her cheek.
Come hide with us from the heat of the day;
Our little home is just over the hay.)

PEACE.

To thee, in all the pride of love,
With welcome from the glorious war,
To thee we come, O Western Dove,
And gather on the shore.
And 'round a glad, enlightened land,
Thy happy millions, hand in hand,
Sing to the God for Whom we stand,
Father of rich and poor.

And all just nations of the earth
Respond and send the truth abroad
That man is of the noblest birth
Who does the will of God.
That nations formed for power alone
Shall tremble when their people groan,

189

Ashes of Roses

For right is higher than the throne,
And stronger than the rod.

Our sin, we hope, is justified.
We waited, but no way was plain.
But ah, remember Him who died;
Remember not the Maine.
Be kind as well as sensitive.
Be great, and let the living live.
It is heroic to forgive;
And mercy leaves no stain.

Then come, ye heroes of the Lord,
Whose bare arm was the last resource,
Go every man and sheathe his sword,
And gear the plow to horse.
Long may thy battleflags be furled,
Bright promise of a better world,
And though a thousand lips be curled,
Still patience be thy force.

Let us forget how well we fought,
And with humiliation see
We, too, have not done all we ought,
Nor been what we should be.
But the gallows leans into the past,
For Mercy hath been heard at last,
And though tradition holds us fast,
All life shall yet be free.

Then let us work to that great day
  When states, and kings, and law, and war
Shall serve their use and pass away,
  And peace shall shut the door.
And men shall face the Eternal Good,
Who then will all be understood,
And we shall stand one common blood,
  No great, no rich, no poor.

MY BROTHER.

I celebrate my brother.   He has come
  From Santiago with the soldier boys.
He hurried forth at sound of fife and drum,
  And now they bring him home.   No foolish noise
Proclaims the hero of our little band.
  He is a private in the Seventy-first,
  Worn with dull service.   When the crowd dispersed
We wept with gratitude, and held his hand,
  And begged him did he hunger, did he thirst,
And soothed his haggard cheek, and stroked his hair.
For he was homesick, and they left him there,
  All in a hot, dead country.   But he bore
All like a man.   My brother.   Our brave boy.
  God bless him, and be with the poorest poor,
Who look with grief upon the nation's joy,
  Thinking of theirs, who shall return no more.

191

Ashes of Roses

ENVOY.

Here ends my record of four happy years.
  Happy? Not always happy. But I see
  How the best fortune that has come to me
Has come in spite of fears.

And I have faltered in the midst of hope.
  Yet smiled. And I am far and quiet now.
It clouds, but there is sunlight on the slope,
  And I am learning how.

I shall not always be what I have been.
  Nor what I am. Nor what I yet shall be.
I shall go on and toil from sin to sin,
  Nor rest till I am free.

Have patience then; dwell not upon my faults;
  I see them all; God knows I am ashamed.
Oh many a night beneath the starry vaults
  I ache for my transgressions; for, unblamed,

I blamed, and sought forbearance. Yet O friends,
  Love me in spite of this, and let us learn
  That the poor souls that toward perfection yearn
Do please the only One Who understands.

www.ingramcontent.com/pod-product-compliance
Lightning Source LLC
Chambersburg PA
CBHW030545040726
47497CB00008B/2581